BLADE

AN MC ROMANCE (OUTLAW SOULS BOOK 4)

HOPE STONE

© Copyright 2020 - All rights reserved.

It is not legal to reproduce, duplicate, or transmit any part of this document in either electronic means or in printed format. Recording of this publication is strictly prohibited and any storage of this document is not allowed unless with written permission from the publisher except for the use of brief quotations in a book review.

This book is a work of fiction. Any resemblance to persons, living or dead, or places, events or locations is purely coincidental.

DEDICATION

This book is dedicated to YOU, the readers and supporters of indie authors like myself. Your posts and kind words on Facebook and Email give me the motivation to keep writing and publishing these stories for you all. Thank you!

Now prepare to escape into the world of The Outlaw Souls MC!

Ready to meet Blade and Kat?...

ONE
KAT

I froze in place as I stepped out the front door of my house and saw that my front tire was flat as a pancake.

"No, no, no," I groaned, hurrying forward to get a closer look as if I could possibly be mistaken.

No luck. It was flat, and I had to deal with it.

"Shit," I hissed under my breath as I threw my purse into the driver's seat and popped the trunk. I was going to kill my brother, Jason. He'd borrowed my car yesterday, and now my perfectly good tire was flat. No way that was a coincidence.

Grabbing the jack, lug wrench, and a spare tire out of the trunk, I hauled them over to the deflated tire. Taking a closer look, I spotted the problem. A nail was stuck in the rubber. I sighed and checked the time on my phone.

There was no way I was going to make it to work on time. *Damn it.*

Firing off a quick text to the owner of the tattoo shop where I worked, I tucked the phone into my back pocket and got to work. Luckily, my dad had taken the time to teach me how to change a tire back when I got my driver's license. It was one of the few bonding experiences we ever had. He said that being a girl was no excuse to not have basic knowledge about your car. So, I knew how to change tires and oil, replace spark plugs, and change the light bulbs in my headlights. I was no mechanic, but at least I felt somewhat independent.

I went through the steps as quickly as I could—loosening the lug nuts, lifting the car with the jack, and taking the flat tire off. I tossed it onto my front porch. Jason didn't know it yet, but he was going to buy me a new one. I put the spare in place and wrapped up the process. It only took about twenty minutes, but I wasn't much of a morning person and was barely going to make it to work on time before this. Now, I was officially behind schedule.

I drove like a bat out of hell through downtown La Playa, weaving in and out of traffic as well as I could on a busy Monday morning. I ignored the dinging of text messages coming through on my phone, knowing it was probably my best friend, wondering where I was.

I dug around blindly in my purse as I kept my eyes on the road. Finally, I felt the unmistakable shape of the pack of gum I stashed there. Pulling the Juicy Fruit out, I unwrapped it, tossing the wrapper onto the floor of the passenger side where it joined a dozen others and empty cans of various energy drinks.

I needed to clean out the car again. It was crazy how quickly it got trashed.

I popped the gum into my mouth, chopping away as the sweet, fruity flavor exploded on my tongue. Pulling into the parking lot of Ink Envy, I took the first parking spot I saw. The shop was a small white building on a corner lot. There was a mural painted along the side of the building, perfectly positioned to catch the eye of drivers along Blackburn Drive. The owner had paid a graffiti artist to create an enticing image. He went with a woman holding a tattoo gun. Coming out of the gun was a rainbow of color that morphed into shapes and images. From left to right, it went from bright and vibrant to dark and striking. It was beautiful, and I still found myself staring at it in awe after working here for nearly three years.

But there was no time to stop and stare today. Locking up my car, I jogged over to the front door of the place, my Chucks eating up distance. I pulled open the door and took two steps before colliding with a tall man's hard body. I went reeling backward with a gasp as the man fumbled with the box in his hands, barely avoiding dropping it onto the linoleum floor.

"Oh, crap. Sorry, Gary," I said as I realized that I had run straight into my coworker. Gary had started working at the shop just a couple of months after I did. He was a talented artist, but not the most reliable person.

Not that I had room to talk on a day that I showed up so late.

"Whatever," he snapped. Brushing past me where I stood in the doorway, he stalked out the door without looking back. I furrowed my brow in confusion.

"What the hell was his problem?" I asked out loud, talking to myself. I was surprised to hear an answer coming from behind me.

"He was just fired."

I turned to see my boss, the owner of the shop, sitting behind the counter to the right side of the room. Brie liked to man the counter herself instead of hiring someone. It made her the face of the business for customers, the first person they would see when walking through the door.

We were in a reception area, where the customers checked in and paid. No one was around, so we could speak freely.

"What happened?" I asked, shocked. Gary wasn't a close friend, not like the other tattoo artist, Piper, who was probably my best friend, but I saw the guy every day. He was a part of my world, and it was jarring to think that he was suddenly gone.

"The guy's a cokehead," Brie said, her voice dripping with disapproval. "I suspected it forever, but his work was good. I was willing to give him the benefit of the doubt until I was refilling supplies this morning and found his stash."

I winced. That was a big no-no.

"Yeah," Brie nodded, reading my oh-shit expression. "He brought that crap into *my* place. He's got balls of steel."

I laughed despite the seriousness of the situation. Brie didn't play around with that stuff. We were sub-contractors, but she was quick to remind us that this was *her* house. She didn't want to get a bad reputation, and drug use by the staff was a quick way to do that.

"Laugh it up, chuckles. You know this leaves us short-handed, right?"

That sobered me up. She had a point. Brie could do tattoos, but her time was usually spent doing other things. She was the only one that did piercings, for instance. That meant that Piper and I were the only full-time tattoo artists. My plate was already full on most days. Piper and I taking over Gary's workload was going to be rough.

"You going to hire someone else?" I asked as I started to make my way to the back of the shop. The area was divided into three sections by a half-wall. We all had curtains hanging from tracks on the ceiling that we could close if a client was getting a tattoo on a private area of their body.

"As soon as possible," she replied. I was almost out of sight when she called out, "Kat?"

"Yeah?" I turned.

"If you still want that piercing, we'll do it before we leave at the end of the day."

I smiled. "Perfect."

Walking into my workspace, I shoved my purse into a cabinet before taking a seat on a stool. I had framed examples of tattoos I'd done up on the wall, as well as a book of basic designs sitting on the counter. It had everything from butterflies to skulls and was useful for people that came in without a concrete idea of what they wanted, which wasn't common.

"Nice of you to show up," Piper said from the workstation beside me. There was a man in her chair, staring at his phone while she tattooed a panther on his shoulder.

"It's Jason's fault. He gave me my car back with a damn nail in the tire. I had to change it out this morning."

"Why did he borrow your car, anyway?" she asked without looking up.

"Because all he has is a bike, and it was raining yesterday. I don't know where he needed to go, but he just kept whining about getting soaked until I gave in."

"You softie."

I chuckled. That might be the first time I was ever called that.

Picking up my trash can, I spit out the gum, which had already lost its flavor. I only chewed it as a deterrent, anyway, trying to kick my stress-induced smoking habit. I knew that cigarettes were terrible for my health, but it was a bad habit that I had picked up as a teenager. I usually only had one or two a day, but I had been attempting to quit for the last month. No more smelling like an ashtray for me.

Brie brought back my first client, a woman I had been working with for the last couple of days. She had come to me to design a massive piece for her entire back. It was a flowering tree, its roots stretched along the base of her spine while the top branches spanned her shoulder blades. Yesterday, I had spent hours outlining the tattoo. Today, we were adding color.

As the client settled into place on my chair with her shirt off, I adjusted the height on my stool until I was comfortable and got to work. The buzzing of my tattoo gun was the only sound in my ears as I lost myself in the work.

I loved when the rest of the world fell away, and I could just create another masterpiece. Some people might not be too impressed with my profession, but I was happy. I considered myself an artist. My canvas was the human body, and my art lasted nearly forever.

My client was a champ, lying still and not even asking for a break. The only time I got a reaction out of her at all was when I was coloring in green leaves along her ribs. She tensed ever so slightly and sucked in a sharp breath.

I couldn't blame her for that. I had a tattoo along the front of my right ribcage—the words *One Life To Live*—so I knew that it was one of the more painful areas to have tattooed.

After three hours, her tattoo was finished, and I snapped a picture of it for my portfolio. I had heard Piper take a couple of Gary's clients while I was working, so I knew that I was going to have to do the same. Taking a break before Brie had a chance to bring someone back for me to work on, I stepped out the back door and popped another piece of gum in my mouth. Pulling out my phone, I fired off a quick text to my brother.

Hey, asshole. You owe me a new tire.

I smirked as I sent it, knowing full well that he was going to try to squirm out of buying it.

Ten minutes passed quickly, and it was time to get back to work. Sure enough, when I stepped inside, Brie was waiting for me with a skinny man that I'd never seen before. I had to try to squeeze him in before my one o'clock appointment. I hated being under pressure like that.

Brie had better find a replacement for Gary soon.

At the end of the day, which was an hour later than usual, I was more than ready for it to be over. I put the finishing touches on a pink hibiscus flower, wiping the ankle tattoo clean as the woman shook with tears in her eyes.

Some people just couldn't handle any amount of pain. They really had no business getting tattoos, but that wasn't my problem. The ones with low pain tolerances had money that was just as green as everyone else's. The only time it bothered me was when the customer kept asking for breaks, and the appointment ran too long.

Putting down my gun, I massaged my aching hand, flexing my fingers.

"Hell of a day, huh?" Piper had already cleaned her tattoo gun and was now sweeping the floor.

"Yeah. I could use a drink. You want to come?" I asked, starting my own cleaning process.

"Where do you want to go?"

I shrugged. "Anywhere but The Pit."

"Come on," Piper whined, leaning against the half wall that separated us. "Xander will be there."

"Yeah, along with all the other Las Balas members. Including my dad."

I did *not* party with my old man. We weren't that close, but I didn't want him to see me tossing back tequila shots or shaking my ass on the dancefloor. It would be weird. My dad was at The Pit nearly every night since it was the hangout of his motorcycle club. Xander was a part of the club, too, and nearly ten years older than Piper. I didn't get the attraction, but I was never into older men. I wasn't going to be a twenty-three-year-old trophy wife. If I ever settled down at all, it would be with someone that was young enough to have some fun and keep up with me in the bedroom.

"Let's go to that place by the beach," I suggested.

"The Copper Bar? I guess that'll be okay. They have daiquiris for two dollars tonight."

"You ladies going out on a Monday night?" Brie asked as she walked through the curtain that divided the front of the shop from the back. "Oh, to be young again."

"Come with us," I said as I took a seat on my stool. Brie was carrying the piercing gun, so I gathered my hair over my right shoulder and tilted my head.

"Please," she rolled her eyes. "If I went out drinking tonight, there's no way I'd be able to drag my happy ass out of bed in the morning."

She chuckled while disinfecting my skin for a tragus piercing. The little piece of cartilage that jutted out over the ear canal was supposed to be one of the most painful piercings you could get, but I didn't mind a little pain. It was all temporary, and, in the end, I reaped the rewards. This time, I was going to have a cute piercing with a dark blue stud that complimented the aquamarine one in my nose.

"You should come," Piper chimed in. "You never know. You might meet a man."

"Oh, now *that's* tempting." Her voice was dripping with sarcasm. I couldn't blame her. Brie had been divorced an astounding four times and vowed that it would never happen again. "Ready, Kat?"

"Go for it."

I sucked in a deep breath as she counted down.

"Three...two...one."

I released my breath through clenched teeth. Then, it was done. I knew it would ache for a while. This particular piercing took a long time to heal.

"You're set. You know the drill. Keep it clean and all that," Brie advised as I checked out the piercing in the mirror.

"Thanks, Brie. You ready for those drinks?" I asked Piper.

"Let's do it."

We left the shop together, getting into my car and heading for the beach. After a long day at work, I was ready for a good time.

TWO
BLADE

"Are you sure about this?" Alex asked as I wrapped the gauze around my hand, covering from the wrist to the knuckles.

"Absolutely," I said, finishing up one hand by applying tape and starting on the other. Behind me, I could hear the jeering and shouting of the crowd surrounding the fight circle, while the two men inside were silent, aside from the dull thud that resulted from their blows to each other's bodies.

"But the odds are four to one against you."

"I know," I smirked. "So, you're going to go put five hundred dollars on me to win."

"What?" Alex looked at me like I was crazy.

I sighed. He'd always been like this, a voice of reason, as he liked to call it. Personally, I thought he needed to let loose a little, but it just wasn't in his nature. Sometimes it drove me nuts, but he was family, so I put up with it. And I'd never tell him, but there were times when he was the voice in my head, talking me down from being too reckless.

"Here." I pulled out the bills that had been rolled up in

my pocket, held together by a rubber band. "Put that down now, before my fight starts. We'll combine the winnings with my payment from the boss and walk out of here twenty-five hundred dollars richer."

"You sound pretty damn sure of yourself."

"I am." I had to be. If I walked into that circle, facing a monster of a man with at least thirty pounds on me, with anything less than full confidence, then I would be doomed before we even began.

Besides, I had no interest in walking away from here a loser.

"Fine, but don't expect me to push your wheelchair around when The Beast is done with you."

"Thanks for your pep talk," I called out after him as he stalked away to place the bet. "Your faith in me helps me to have faith in myself."

The only response I got was the middle finger thrown over his shoulder, which made me break out into loud laughter. It was perfect, just what I needed to cut through the tension before the fight.

I was new to street fighting, and this was only my third time here. My friend, Rick, had told me about the gig. He had been coming here for months, making decent money and, more importantly, working out some aggression. That was the main reason I kept coming. Sure, the money was nice, but I was more interested in working out my issues with my fists. I thought of it as nontraditional therapy. It was a hell of a lot better than nothing.

Rick had to work tonight, so I asked my cousin to tag along instead. The one thing I knew for sure was it was best not to come alone. Each win paid out a thousand bucks, and it wouldn't be out of the question for someone alone to be jumped by some of the men around here to get the cash.

The current fight ended, so I got to my feet. I did a few quick stretches, ending with cracking my neck. Despite my lack of street fighting experience, I was no stranger to a fight. As the only son of an army general, I was pushed to join up my entire life. My father even went so far as to insist that I attend military school and receive hand-to-hand combat training as a teenager.

I didn't know if he thought that would somehow motivate me to follow in his footsteps, but it didn't work. I hated the strict structure and emphasis on discipline. My father wasn't happy, and I didn't think our relationship ever recovered, but I decided quickly that I wasn't soldier material. It didn't take long to get kicked out of the place, but I had picked up some fighting skills by then. Over the years, I'd honed those skills in bar fights and a general knack for finding trouble.

"You ready?" Alex asked as he returned.

I just nodded before turning and starting to make my way through the crowd. They parted for me, many of them shouting taunting insults until I reached the edge of the circle, the boundary of which was marked with white spray paint on the concrete floor.

This warehouse was one of many old and abandoned ones on this side of town. The windows were boarded up, and the only entrance was a sliding metal door at the back of the building that had previously been a loading area for large trucks. It helped the guys running this place to keep track of who came and went, but it also meant there wasn't an easy getaway if we were ever busted. So, I hoped it never came to that.

On the other side of the crudely drawn barrier, I saw my opponent, a man that had earned the nickname The Beast with both his size and manner, stepping through the crowd on the other side. I could feel the buzz of anticipation in the air as the crowd got worked up for the fight. I knew that we were the main event of the evening. The new guy who was making a name for himself around here versus a man that was known for being big and mean. He wasn't undefeated, but he didn't lose often, either. I took his measure from twenty feet away.

The Beast wasn't much taller than me, but I had to admit that he was bigger. It wasn't all muscle, either. The two of us were both shirtless, and I could see that he was carrying extra weight around his middle. That could work to his advantage if he got me pinned beneath him.

Despite his extra weight, his shoulders were broad, and it was clear he didn't skip arm day at the gym. There was no doubt that he was strong. I was sure to get pummeled if he got his hands on me.

So, I had to make sure that didn't happen.

"Ladies and gentlemen," a voice rang out from my left. Turning, I saw the man in charge, Luca Bianchi, shouting to be heard above the crowd. "We've come to our last fight of the evening. Place your bets now. Will it be the up and coming biker, Blade?"

There was a smattering of hoots and cheers, but not much. It was a good thing I didn't care about that. It worked to my advantage to be underestimated.

"Or will it be the meanest son of a bitch I know, The Beast?"

This response from the crowd was much more impressive, and the idiot loved it. Throwing his hands into the air, he stepped into the middle of the ring, gesturing for them to cheer louder for him as if their support mattered at all.

It didn't. All that mattered was who was better in the ring. Tonight that would be me.

I was strong, with six-pack abs and my own sculpted biceps, but what would give me the edge in this fight was my speed. While The Beast was busy working the crowd, I stepped into the ring and circled around him. I stayed on the balls of my feet, making sure that I was at his back as he moved, just waiting for the signal to begin.

Finally, a shrill whistle cut through the air, and I ran forward, reaching my opponent before he even had a chance to figure out where I'd gone. A quick jab to the kidney made him let out a whoosh of air, but I was gone before he could react, facing him on the other side of our circle.

Most of the crowd around us booed, and I couldn't keep the smirk off my face. A lot of assholes were about to lose the money they bet against me.

The Beast let out a noise that I could only describe as a growl, his face turning red as he moved toward me. Anger was going to be his weakness. I moved out of his path quickly, landing a kick to the side of his knee as I went. His leg buckled, but he managed to straighten it out and stay on his feet.

A small part of me was glad that he didn't go down easy. I wanted a challenging fight.

I could sense the moment that The Beast started taking me seriously. When his eyes met mine again, the anger was still there, but I could also see a calculating look. He didn't move without thinking again.

Good. Now we could really begin.

The sounds of the crowd around us faded into the background as I became laser-focused on the huge man in front of me. Time dragged on as the fight got more intense. The only rule here was no weapons, so there was nothing that was off-limits.

I stuck to my strategy of quick jabs while staying out of reach, but The Beast had a long reach and was able to land a few blows. I had a couple of bruised ribs and a busted lip, but it wasn't going to slow me down.

The longer the fight went on, the more I tapped into my inner darkness, the anger and guilt that I had carried with me for ten years. It fueled me, making me more vicious. I barely felt the pain of the hits I had taken, and I got more daring, able to land several blows to the man's face. I even broke his nose.

Then, he got a hold of me. I knew that it might happen, and all I could do was hope that I'd inflicted enough damage to take him down. I took blows to my sides, trying to block them as well as I could with my arms, but it was the right hook to the temple that sent me reeling. I saw stars.

Stumbling back two steps, I couldn't get away from him, so I tapped into every ounce of aggression that I had. Bringing my arms up, I blocked his next blow. It brought him even further into my space, and, reacting on instinct, I brought my elbow across his face with all my strength. He was dazed, so I swiped his legs. It hurt my own shin, but he went down. Hard.

The sound of him hitting the concrete was a dull thud, and he didn't get back up. I stood over him, my chest heaving as I wiped blood away from my chin.

I barely registered the surprised reaction of the people around me as I walked out of the ring. Alex was at my side, and he wordlessly handed me a bottle of beer. I took a swig, savoring the cold liquid as it slid down my throat.

"Are you okay?" Alex was eyeing my lip, and I wondered just how bad it looked.

"I'll live."

"And you're lucky for that. That guy was a monster."

"I think he prefers to be called a beast."

"How can you make jokes after such a brutal fight?"

I shrugged. The truth was, I felt great. My adrenaline was still pumping, and I had let out some of my ever-present anger. Street fighting was a hell of an outlet.

"Let's pick up my money and head to the Blue Dog," I said. "I could use about five more of these."

I held up the beer bottle, then took another big swallow.

Alex didn't say anything else about the fight, but I knew that he had something on his mind. Everyone was starting to leave, with the few winners making their way to Luca's man, Gino, who handled the betting. I went to Luca first, collecting my winnings.

"I gotta say, you surprised me out there," he said while chewing on a toothpick and counting out my payment in twenty-dollar bills. "I can count on one hand the number of times someone has taken down The Beast."

"Yeah, well, don't be afraid to take a chance on the underdog next time," I advised.

I only got a grunt in response. Alex and I collected the money we won, and I pulled my black t-shirt back on, as well as my black leather jacket. Then, I tossed my empty beer bottle in a trash barrel on my way out the door.

The night air was crisp, as it had gotten colder when the sun went down. It was springtime, and the trees were just starting to get their leaves back.

"You wanna tell me what's on your mind?" I asked as we got into Alex's pickup truck. It was one of the nicest vehicles in the parking lot.

Alex worked as the foreman for a commercial construction company in nearby Trotter Beach, so he made good money, and it showed in his choice of vehicle. He was lucky no one broke into the thing in this neighborhood.

"Why are you doing this?" he asked, looking at me with tired eyes.

"The fighting?"

I leaned back against the leather seat and felt my aching ribs. They hurt, but I was pretty sure none of them were cracked.

"Yes, the fighting," Alex responded impatiently. "Don't you see how dangerous this shit is? What if the big bastard had knocked you down, fracturing your skull on the concrete? Do you think your friends in there would have called an ambulance for you?"

No.

"I don't have friends in there." I shot him a smile. "That's why I brought you."

He didn't look amused. "Yeah, well, it's a one and done for me. I know you're really fighting your own demons, but there's got to be a healthier way to do that."

I shook my head and looked out the window. There was a long moment of silence between us, but I eventually broke it.

"What the hell would you have me do? Go to some headshrinker?"

The idea was laughable. I wasn't the sharing type, especially with some stranger. The fighting worked for me. I didn't need to talk about my damn feelings.

"I think they prefer the term therapist."

Alex pulled into the parking lot of the Blue Dog, and I was eager to get inside the bar. Even this conversation with Alex hadn't brought me down from the high of winning, and I wanted to enjoy it. The Outlaw Souls were inside, and as a prospective member of the motorcycle club, I belonged among them. I stepped out of the truck, but when I turned to close the door, I saw that Alex hadn't moved.

"You're not coming?"

He shook his head. "I'm not in the mood tonight. Get one of your biker friends to give you a ride home."

I shut the door of his truck, and Alex left before I even made it across the parking lot. I knew he wasn't happy with me, but he'd get over it. I was sure he'd come again if I needed him to have my back. So, I brushed off his concerns and walked into the bar, where I could start spending my winnings.

looked begrudging as he answered my questions. I trailed my eyes down to his hand and saw that he was carrying a white plastic bag at his side. "And as for what happened in there, I think you meant to thank me.'"

I sighed, breaking eye contact. He was right. I was embarrassed about the whole thing, but I still owed him some gratitude.

"Thank you."

"You're welcome," he said. Blade started walking backward toward his bike so that he could still speak to me as he walked away. "It's okay to need help sometimes, tough girl."

I didn't have a response to that. He'd helped me out back there, and I didn't want to fight with him right now. So, I turned around and walked away, deciding to buy my paint from somewhere else on another day.

drew me to you in the first place." He took a step closer to me until he was so close that he could reach out and touch me. "All I want is to touch you, Kat. Get a little payback for those drinks I bought you."

I clenched my teeth and met his eyes. "I don't owe you anything."

"Is there a problem here?" a voice asked from behind David, and he turned, revealing a pissed off looking Blade.

"Not at all," David said, his voice oily as he stepped away from me.

Blade's hands were fisted at his side, and his breathing was heavy. I had a feeling that he was trying to decide if he should pound David into a pulp or not.

"It's fine, Blade," I said, scooping up the contents of my purse and shoving them back inside. "I'm done with this place, anyway."

As I side-stepped David, I thought for a moment that he might be dumb enough to try to stop me, but he didn't. He just glowered at me as I went by. Blade kept his eyes pinned on the skeezy asshole until I had walked past them both, heading for the door.

"You keep your hands to yourself from now on," I heard him say to David. The threat was so clear in his voice that I felt a shiver go down my spine, even though it wasn't directed at me.

I pushed open the door to go outside and felt his presence behind me. As I got to the parking lot, I spun around to face him.

"You didn't have to do that, you know. What were you even doing here? Did you follow me?"

"Hell no. I'm not a stalker. I came to the closest hardware store to the Blue Dog to pick up a couple of packs of lightbulbs. The one in the men's bathroom went out." He

"No?" I was confused by the question. Hadn't he just stopped me to say hello?

"I saw you put something inside of your purse."

"Yeah, paint samples."

"I'm not so sure about that. You seem like the dishonest type."

"*Excuse me?*" White-hot anger flared to life inside of me.

"I'm going to need to search your bag."

"No way. What's your problem?"

"You know, you seem like a woman that makes bad decisions. Like leaving a perfectly nice guy on the dance floor after leading him on, only to run off with a guy that looks like he belongs behind bars."

"You know, men that refer to themselves as *nice guys* rarely are," I told him, walking over to the unmanned customer service counter nearby and unceremoniously dumping the contents of my purse all over the place just to be petulant. His insults of both Blade and me pissed me off, so I didn't care if I seemed childish.

My wallet, gum, and birth control pills went spilling out all over the place, as well as all the color swatches I'd put in there. David pursed his lips as he saw that I hadn't stolen anything. Then, he smiled.

"You know, I should probably search you, just in case."

My skin crawled. What. A. Creep.

"No fucking way," I said loudly, drawing attention from the other customers nearby.

"Then, maybe I should call the police?"

Did he really think that would scare me? Pathetic.

"Go ahead, but you'll also have to call an ambulance if you try to lay a finger on me."

David laughed. "I knew you'd be fiesty. It was what

such an insatiable need for a man before. Of course, it had to happen with the wrong guy.

I could really use another cigarette. It was too bad that I threw the pack I bought away when my commitment to kick the habit returned.

Embracing the idea of a distraction, I went to the hardware store to look through paint samples, choosing to focus on something productive instead of my confusing feelings for Blade. There were so many color options that I was almost immediately overwhelmed. I knew I didn't want the ugly pinkish color that had been on the wall, but other than that, I was lost.

Grabbing a couple of swatches of each color I might be even remotely interested in, I shoved them into my purse. When I got home, I'd tape them to the wall and see what I liked best with the living room's lighting.

I was heading to the door when I was stopped. A man in the blue polo shirt that all the employees wore stepped into my path. His name tag listed him as a manager, but all of that was secondary as I realized that I knew the man, sort of.

"David?" I felt a twinge of guilt as I remembered leaving him on the dance floor when Blade showed up, then blowing him off when I came back inside after having sex in the alley. I knew that I didn't owe the guy anything, but I could tell that he was disappointed. I didn't want to be a bitch, but I wasn't really feeling it *before* Blade showed up. After he made his appearance, it was unthinkable to go home with David.

"Kat, how...*interesting* to see you here." There was something in his voice that I didn't like. He seemed cold somehow. "Do you know why I've stopped you from leaving?"

NINETEEN
KAT

I was finished with my mother's room. The space had a new paint job and decor. It was now a guest bedroom. I stood in the room after making the bed and felt a lightness in my heart that I hadn't thought would come for a long time. It hurt to let her go, but I was finally ready to start moving past it.

Next, I was redecorating the living room. My mom had painted the room a salmon color when we moved in years ago, back when I was still in diapers. I'd never liked it because it was too girly for me, so now I was going to change it.

I felt like I was changing my life as I changed my house. I was in the best place emotionally that I had been since my mom died. Then, I thought about Blade and decided that might be bullshit. Why couldn't I move on from this guy? He was trouble for me, with his Outlaw Souls patch on his back.

But I'd slept with him on Tuesday at the bar, and I couldn't stop thinking about doing it again. I'd never had the unmistakable sound of motorcycles starting. I hurried forward, coming around the bushes to see who was there, just as two motorcycles took off in the opposite direction, following an unpaved road that would lead them back to La Playa. I wasn't able to see who the riders were, but there was no disguising the patches on the back of their jackets.

"Las Balas," I murmured.

"God damn it," Trainer said from beside me. "They were spying on us."

"You think they knew what we were doing?"

"There's no way they do, but it's still not good news. This shitty situation just got even more complicated."

I couldn't help but think of Kat. She'd heard a snippet of Ryder talking about what we were doing here tonight. Did she hear enough to send her Las Balas buddies to watch us, or was it just coincidence?

I hated feeling suspicious of her, but she'd made it clear that Las Balas were her people. I would have to talk to her about it, and I hoped like hell that I was wrong.

The metal detector in my hand made a noise, and the readout indicated there was steel beneath my feet. I got excited for a second before I heard Trainer's detector going off to my far left.

Right, there could be more than one piece of steel here. It was impossible to know what was underground. Shaking up my paint can, I marked a big red X on the grass and continued onward. I wasn't into spending much time in nature, but I could appreciate the beauty of this place. The sky was colorful as the sun started to set, and the breeze in the air made the tall grass and trees sway.

We kept at it until it was fully dark outside, but we hadn't even covered half of the property yet. It was that big.

"I'll come back out tomorrow night with Chalupa, Kim, and Swole," Ryder said as we met back up at his truck. Hawk packed away the metal detectors again while he talked.

"Then comes the fun task of digging," Trainer said drily.

"You got it," Ryder agreed. "Now, let's get back to the Blue Dog. The first round's on me."

That sounded pretty good to me, and so we hopped on our bikes, ready to follow his truck back to the bar, but a movement from nearby caught my eye.

"Hey, wait a minute," I said, lowering my kickstand and hopping off the bike.

"What is it?" Trainer asked.

"Someone over there," I pointed in the direction that I'd seen what I was sure was the outline of a man. "Behind that tall shrubbery."

"You sure?" Trainer asked, getting off his own bike.

"Yeah. Someone's watching us."

As soon as those words were out of my mouth, we heard

were hidden. The thing was heavier than I expected it to be, and I wasn't looking forward to lugging it around for the next few hours.

"We only have four of these things, so we're going to start at the south end of the property and spread out to work our way north. If you detect something, mark it with a red X on the grass," Ryder spoke as Pin passed out the paint cans. "We'll come back through later and dig."

There was a small group of us tonight, and a second group would come tomorrow, that way we didn't push anyone too much. The days were getting longer, so the sun wouldn't be fully set for about three hours. Plenty of time to cover a lot of ground.

My mind lingered on Kat while I walked with the metal detector. Today, work had been more of the same. She ignored me or was hostile, and I found my frustration mounting. As expected, she didn't change her attitude just because we had sex outside the bar. In fact, she seemed even more determined to push me away, as if my presence was a bigger problem for her now. If she thought she was going to get me to quit my job just because she decided to back the wrong horse, she was dead wrong.

Most of the land was flat, any trees that had previously been here being cleared out so that houses could be built on top of it. In the distance, we could see subdivisions being built, the same few cookie-cutter designs repeated over and over in various shades of tan, yellow, or blue, all sitting way too close to each other. I'd lived in places like this growing up, with their HOAs and everybody in each other's business. I hated it.

Looking around, it was obvious that Raymond was holding onto this land for a reason. There were houses sprouting up everywhere on the lots surrounding this one.

But when I turned back around, I knew that I'd never reach that point. I'd always want her.

Fuck Las Balas. Fuck her dad. Fuck this whole shitty situation.

"Get back inside," I told her. There was really nothing else to say. I could read the indecision in her expression, but somehow I knew that Kat wasn't going to change her mind about me. I was still the enemy in her eyes, and she was too damn stubborn to consider otherwise. Which just made me angry all over again.

"I'm on the pill," she said.

Fuck. I'd been so caught up in my desire for her that I hadn't even stopped to think about that.

"Good." I started to walk down the alley so that I could go around the building to where my bike was parked. I didn't need to go back inside. I'd gotten what I came for. Turning back to her after a couple of feet, I called out, "Kitten?"

She paused with her hand outstretched to open the metal back door. "Yeah?"

"Don't even think of going home with anyone else tonight."

I knew that it was an unreasonable demand, but I didn't give a shit. To my surprise, she didn't argue. She just flashed me a little smirk before disappearing inside.

"OKAY, you hold the metal detector like this, with the round part pointed at the ground. I've programmed the readout to let you know if it detects steel."

Hawk was passing out metal detectors to each of us as we stood on the edge of the property where the weapons to the side and lined myself up at her entrance. I thrust inside of her wet heat. It was raw and rough, with an added thrill of knowing that we were in public, even if it was dark here.

I took her hard against the back wall of the bar, fulfilling a need that we both didn't want to admit we had. Kat's ankles hooked together behind my back, and she clung to my shoulders. I buried my face in her neck, breathing in the flowery scent of her hair.

God, she was so tight in this position, and her breathy moans were driving me wild. I'd never been so uninhibited with a woman, and the gritty nature of our sex meant that I was barreling toward an orgasm quickly. But I wouldn't finish until she got what she needed out of this, too.

With her dress pushed up around her waist, the bare globes of her perfect ass were exposed, so I grabbed them with my hands and squeezed while I directed her up and down on my cock. I took her mouth again, nipping at her lower lip.

Kat shrieked into my mouth as she came, her inner channel gripping my erection and sending shockwaves of pleasure through my body. I pulled my mouth away from hers as I reached my own climax, barking out her name like it was a curse as I exploded inside of her.

It was so damn good, and I had a feeling this quickie wasn't going to be nearly enough. Whether Kat considered us enemies or not, our sexual chemistry was too much to ignore. I disengaged our bodies and lowered her until her feet were back on the ground. I turned away as I zipped my pants back up and she righted her dress. When I'd pulled her out here, I'd hoped that afterward, the lust that I felt for her would be gone.

EIGHTEEN
BLADE

I probably shouldn't have come to the bar. It wasn't in my plans for the night. In fact, I didn't have any plans and probably would have ended up at the Blue Dog. So, when I heard Kat and Piper talking about coming to the Copper Bar tonight and meeting men, I talked myself into following them.

I couldn't explain my reasoning, but when I arrived and saw Kat on the dance floor in a skimpy dress with some asshole's hands on her, I didn't stop to think before I acted. I knew that whatever had started between us was over now, but then she rubbed her body against mine, making me hard as a diamond. Now my tongue was in her mouth as she kneaded my ass with her fingers.

I was under no delusions that this would change anything, but that wasn't going to stop me. If anything, I was fueled by my anger at her. It needed an outlet, and I was going to take it. Reaching down, I unbuttoned my pants and pulled out my cock. Lifting her legs, I put them around my waist while her back was braced against the building. I broke our kiss and looked into her eyes as I pulled her thong frown on his face. I gave him an apologetic smile before I was pulled out of the backdoor of the bar. We were in a poorly lit alley between the bar and a brick building behind it, with no one around.

"Are you looking for trouble here, Kitten?" Blade asked.

The fresh air cleared my head a little, and I felt a flicker of irritation. "I told you not to call me that."

Blade moved closer to me until my back was pressed up against the vinyl siding of the bar. He didn't stop until I was caged in by his arms, and I couldn't seem to catch my breath. The heat radiating from him seeped into me, and I couldn't hold myself back anymore.

I reached up to grab the sides of his face and pulled his lips to mine. I could blame it on the alcohol, but that wasn't really why I did it. As Blade took control of the kiss, I knew that I needed to be with him one more time.

My head swam once I was on my feet, all the alcohol that I'd consumed quickly taking effect and making everything seem somehow more vibrant and muted at the same time.

"Let's dance," I said, grabbing David's hand and leading him to the dance floor.

My long hair was down, and I whipped it around as I closed my eyes and let my body move to the music. David was with me, and I could feel his cautious touch as his hands rested on my hips. The music was coming from big speakers on each side of the stage, and the volume was so cranked up that I couldn't even hear myself think. The heavy bass made my bones vibrate.

Suddenly, there was another set of hands on me, pulling me back into a hard body. My eyes flew open, but I knew who it was before I even saw him. It was clear in the way that every nerve ending in my body lit up like a firework. A rolling heat that was shockingly similar to the warmth I got from my tequila shot licked up my spine, and I arched my back so that my ass was pressed into Blade's erection. I loved knowing that I got him so worked up.

"What the hell, man?" David said, stepping forward.

"Back off, All-American. She wants *me*."

I did, and my hazy mind couldn't seem to hold onto the good reasons why I shouldn't. I turned around in his arms and looked up at him. The lighting in here was dim, but I could see him clearly. His eyes were burning into mine, and he looked almost angry.

That shouldn't make me hot for him, but it did.

"What are you doing here?" I asked, but he couldn't hear me over the music.

The next thing I knew, I was being led off the dance floor. I glanced back to see David watching me go with a school football team and homecoming king. He just gave off that vibe.

Not my type, but if I could avoid handing over my cash, I would. Besides, I wanted to go home with someone tonight to get this need for Blade out of my system, and the guy that looked nothing like him was probably a good candidate.

"Thanks," I said with a smile. "I'm Kat."

"David." He held out his hand, and I shook it. There was no electricity between us, but I didn't have to have that with every guy I slept with, right?

"You with the party?" I asked.

"Yeah, it's my friend's birthday, so we figured we'd grab a few drinks."

He spoke as if they were stepping outside the box by coming here. I wondered if it was because it was a seedy bar or if the day of the week was the issue.

"So, that's why you're here, buying me drinks?" I asked with a flirty smile. "Figured you'd take a walk on the wild side to celebrate this special occasion?"

"I'd like to." He smiled, and I saw two rows of perfectly straight, white teeth.

I sipped my drink while we talked. It was nice and strong, exactly how I liked it. Which was good, because David might be physically perfect, but he was dull, and after making small talk with him for ten minutes, I needed the alcohol to keep enjoying myself.

I looked around and found that Piper was on the dancefloor, grinding between two guys that were also a part of David's group. I finished off my drink and ordered another shot, enjoying the way the burn of the alcohol seemed to spread through my whole body. I slammed the empty shot glass down onto the bar and got off the barstool. The dress I was wearing rode up my thighs, but I didn't fix it.

but if he is a part of that, I don't want anything to do with him."

The truth was, I felt conflicted, but it was easier to shun Blade than to turn my back on everything I'd ever known. It was driving me crazy to be near him, and I turned that into anger. I could deal with anger, but this needy desire that I *still* harbored for the guy was another story.

Piper took us by her apartment before we went to the bar so that she could change into something more suited for picking up men. I wasn't worried about that, but she shoved a little black dress into my hands and insisted I put it on. I agreed, pulling it over my head, and checking myself out in the mirror, I saw it fell down about mid-thigh and looked good with my boots. I liked it.

When we went to the Copper Bar, it was busier than I expected for a Tuesday night. The parking lot was half-full, and we walked inside to see that there was a large group of people that had pushed a bunch of tables together. They seemed to be celebrating something, and most of them were men.

I went straight to the bar, ordering a shot and a Long Island iced tea. I tossed back the tequila, not bothering with the lime chaser. Piper ordered herself a drink beside me, sticking to beer.

"Starting off kind of strong, aren't you?" She asked.

"I'm here to drink."

"Then, allow me to buy that for you," said a man's voice from behind me.

I swiveled the barstool around to see a tall man with wavy blonde hair and blue eyes standing there. He looked like a representation of the perfectly typical white, American man. He was probably the quarterback of his high

"We'll take my car," Piper suggested.

"Sure," I agreed.

I didn't care either way. I just needed a stiff drink. Maybe it would help keep me from giving in and smoking again. I really did attribute my falling off the wagon to Blade. Knowing that I had to work so closely with him was stressing me out. I was trying to cling to my anger with him to keep myself from focusing on how much I was still attracted to him. Sitting ten feet away from each other for most of the day was not making that easy.

"So, today was...*interesting*," Piper said once we were inside of her car. The door of the shop opened just as we were leaving the parking lot, and Blade's customer walked out.

"That's one way to put it."

"Help me understand what's going on here. You guys aren't the Capulets and the Montagues, you know."

"That doesn't mean we aren't enemies," I sighed. "I'm choosing a side in a war between these two clubs. I'm backing Las Balas."

"Why? We both know how secretive they are. We don't really know what they get up to."

"Because my dad's in the club," I said, avoiding her eyes. If anyone knew about the strained relationship I had with the man, it was Piper.

"And someone has to be the bad guy in this story. You don't want it to be him." It wasn't a question.

"He's not always a good guy. I know that," I said. "But I've heard that Outlaw Souls kill people. They don't just attack Las Balas, they are a plague in La Playa with their drug running and the other shit they get up to. My dad always told me growing up that they were like a gang terrorizing the town. Blade can be as charming as he wants,

SEVENTEEN
KAT

"Come out with me," I insisted as Piper and I were leaving for the day. The shop was technically closed even though Blade was still finishing up a tattoo with a client. So, the two of us were taking off while Blade and Brie stayed behind.

"What did you have in mind?" she asked as we both waved goodbye to Brie. Piper had bid Blade a good night while I said nothing.

"Let's go to the Copper Bar again. I liked that place. And maybe you'll get lucky enough to find a man worth bringing home again."

"Or maybe you will," she said.

I pulled open the door of the shop and let her walk through first. I couldn't imagine finding anyone to take home tonight. My mind strayed to the hot night I'd spent with Blade. His big hands knew exactly how to touch me to bring out all the pleasure I needed, and his full lips set me on fire.

Damn it. I didn't want to find him physically attractive anymore, but it turned out that it was something I couldn't just turn off.

"Neither am I," I said, and Ryder looked at me questioningly. I didn't think now was the time to elaborate on my relationship with Kat, but I knew I'd need to fill him in later. As much as it felt like a private thing, I knew that it wasn't anymore. It could affect the club.

Kat huffed before getting up and walking to the front of the shop. After a moment, I heard her talking to Brie like nothing was wrong. She had just been trying to get away from me.

It was amazing how different this job felt now. Working closely with Kat didn't feel like such a blessing anymore. It was more like being trapped in a cage with a wild animal that was likely to bite my head off at any moment.

I went back to working on Ryder's tattoo, and he watched my work in silence. In the end, the tattoo turned out great, but I couldn't say if it was worth the headache.

"Meet at the Blue Dog tomorrow night at seven," he said. "We could only get four metal—"

"Maybe we should talk about that later," I interrupted him. I glanced over at Kat, and she was sitting perfectly still. I didn't want to think that she'd run and tell her dad or brother what we were up to, but her behavior the last couple of days made me think that she would. If nothing else, just to spite me.

Ryder's eyes followed mine, and he once again scrutinized Kat. She must have felt his eyes on her because she looked up with narrowed eyes.

"What?"

"Do I know you?" Ryder asked. "You look familiar to me. I just can't place you."

"I'm Kat Maddox."

"Maddox? As in Clint Maddox?"

"That's my father."

I saw the hardening of the lines in Ryder's face. He obviously knew that her dad was in Las Balas. Kat must have thought that he would do something to her despite our conversation outside because her next words were defensive.

"Don't even think about laying a hand on me, though. You'll bring down a lot of trouble on yourself."

"I wouldn't," Ryder said, but he sounded pretty damn unhappy. "We have a code of honor. Las Balas are the ones that go after families. They did it to me."

"I don't believe you."

I almost felt sorry for her.

"That's your problem," I told her. "You won't even consider that you're wrong."

"My dad isn't a bad guy," she said, and for once, I could hear doubt in her voice.

happen. He took a seat in the chair and held his arm on the armrest so that I could reach the area where he wanted the tattoo.

"Well, you should probably appoint someone to be your vice president. That would help with the club matters."

"You asking for the spot?"

"Hell no," I said, taking a seat on the stool. "I haven't been in the club long enough for that."

Ryder smiled as he leaned back in the chair and got comfortable. "You're right about that, but down the road? I could see you working your way up into an officer position. You've got the right stuff."

From her spot ten feet away, Kat made a huffing noise that I thought was supposed to indicate disbelief. Or maybe humor. I ignored it, but Ryder looked over. I saw him eyeing Kat curiously for a moment, and a completely stupid feeling of possession came over me.

"Anyway," I drew his attention back to me. "I did a mock-up of what we discussed. Is this what you had in mind?"

I showed him a page in my sketchbook of a skeletal head in black and white clutching a blood-red rose between its teeth.

"That's it," Ryder confirmed. "Maybe just a little smaller, because I want it here."

He pointed to a spot just below the crease of his elbow. I grabbed a pen and drew the outline on his skin.

"That looks great," he said when I was done.

"Okay. Relax, and we'll get started."

Ryder was unphased by the tattoo gun. He relaxed back into the seat and even closed his eyes for a while. I almost thought he might be asleep until he spoke.

Ryder was here. "And I have a feeling it's about to get worse."

"Who is that?"

"Ryder."

"Ryder Hernandez? The president of the Outlaw Souls?"

"The one and only." I reached over, took the cigarette from her hand, and took a puff.

Kat snatched it away from me, shaking her head.

"What's he doing here? Has he come to threaten me?"

"What? Of course not. Jesus, what kind of people do you think we are?"

Kat didn't answer, just tossed her cigarette butt on the ground and crushed it with the heel of her boot.

"He's here for a tattoo."

"Then let's get in there."

I pulled open the door, letting Kat walk in ahead of me. She plopped herself down on her stool while I headed to the front, just as Ryder walked in.

"Hey, man," I greeted him. "Come on back."

Piper had her curtain pulled, and I knew that she was giving a tattoo to a woman that wanted a tribal design that started on her back and wrapped around her ribcage, right under her breasts. It was going to take a while, but it sounded like it would be an impressive piece.

Kat didn't have a customer right now, so she was playing on her phone. Or at least pretending to be. I had a feeling that her ears were wide open.

"Thanks for fitting me in. I'm so damn busy these days, but I had time today."

Ryder took off his jacket, and I carefully hung it up for him. It was part of the club rules that the patch could never touch the ground, so I needed to make sure that didn't

When I was finished, the customer paid Brie and left. The second the door closed behind him, Kat scoffed.

"So, are you trying to get new recruits for Outlaw Souls or something?"

I sighed, already sick of this game. "What are you talking about?"

"Just the way you were talking to that guy, going on and on about bikes and riding, mentioning that other guy. I recognize his name. I know he's a member, too."

"Trainer's our Road Captain and a hell of a good guy."

"Says you."

"Says his wife and kids."

Something in Kat's face softened for just a moment, but it was gone so quickly that I started to question if I imagined it.

"Whatever," she rolled her eyes. "I'm taking a break."

Grabbing her purse, she stood and walked out the back door of the tattoo shop. I hesitated for a second before deciding that I wasn't done talking and followed her. To my surprise, I found her leaning up against the side of the building, lighting up a cigarette.

"I didn't know you smoked," I said, earning myself another glare.

"I don't," she replied while exhaling a cloud of smoke.

"Could have fooled me."

She rolled her eyes. "I quit a month ago. You're witnessing a relapse. Hell, you're causing it."

"Don't you think you might be overreacting?"

"You know what bothers me? You act like I'm the only one with a problem."

"No, we both have a problem." The sound of a motorcycle drew my attention to the street, and I realized that

I turned back to Kat to see her glowering at me. "See, I didn't poison them, no matter what you think of me. Do you want one, Kitten?"

"Don't call me that," she hissed.

She looked pissed now. I had been trying to get under her skin, to get a rise out of her because I was angry about yesterday, but I had a feeling that using my nickname for her had been a step too far. I hadn't even meant to say it, it just slipped out. Grabbing a maple bar out of the box, I shoved half of it into my mouth before tossing the box onto the counter in her workspace.

"Help yourself," I said through a mouthful of pastry.

I went into my section and sat on the stool, but I didn't close the curtains, not today. I wasn't going to let her anger at me keep me hidden while I was here. Apparently, she had the same idea because her curtains stayed open as well, and we were both forced to act like the other person didn't exist. It was awkward, but I blamed Kat for it. She was the one that was angry just because I was an Outlaw Soul. I didn't like her connection to Las Balas, and it probably wasn't a good idea to keep seeing each other, but I wasn't the one being an asshole here.

Kat didn't touch the damn donuts, which drove me crazy. I knew she wanted one. Why did she have to be so stubborn?

I had a client come in not long after that, and I gave him my full attention, hoping that a good distraction would make this situation better. His tattoo was a cross on his shoulder with angel wings behind it stretching out on either side. As I worked, we made small talk, and I discovered that he was a rider, as well. It made the time go quicker as we found that common ground, and I told him all about my Sporster and the work that Trainer had done on it.

"She must have been pretty upset about the death of her husband at the hands of the mob."

"She was, but you know how strong women can be. They compartmentalize that shit. Right now, she wants the stash off the land for the safety of her and her kid."

"When do we start?"

"Two days. Hawk will have his hands on a few metal detectors by then."

"Count me in."

"Good." He racked his knuckles on the table twice and stood. "I'll see you tomorrow afternoon."

"Tomorrow?"

"My tattoo?"

"Oh, yeah." I nodded. "Right. See you tomorrow."

I had forgotten all about that. Now Ryder was going to be in the shop with Kat, who apparently hated us.

This was going to be interesting.

"WHAT'S THAT?" Kat asked with an annoyed look on her face for no good reason. It was first thing in the morning, and I had just walked into the tattoo shop carrying a flat white box.

"Donuts," I said with a big grin. I knew that she had a sweet tooth but wouldn't want to eat something that I'd brought in. Basically, I was fucking with her. "Want one?"

"I do," Piper chimed in. I held the box out to her, and she selected a jelly-filled one.

"Brie, do you want a donut?" I called out to her at the front counter.

"Always," she said, coming in to grab a classic glazed one.

It was caddy-corner to the Blue Dog, so it was no surprise to walk in and see other Outlaw Souls there. I nodded at Yoda and Ryder, who were sitting across from each other in a booth, but I sat alone at a table in the back. I didn't feel much like socializing tonight.

I knew that it was pointless to think about Kat. I barely knew her, but it was a bitter disappointment that things were over so quickly. If nothing else, she was good in bed, and I would have liked to go another couple rounds.

Fuck it.

I was just going around in circles here. The fact was that we had discovered an insurmountable difference between us; Kat had even called us enemies.

I was facing the door, so I saw when a group of women entered the restaurant. One of them had long dark hair, and it reminded me of Kat so much that I made myself look away. God, I was acting like a lovesick teenager. It was ridiculous. Kat was just a good lay, I told myself firmly, still avoiding looking at the woman that could have been her sister with all their similarities. I felt a presence approaching and looked up, expecting the waitress. Instead, I saw Ryder there.

"Got a minute?" he asked.

"Sure," I said unenthusiastically.

Ryder sat across from me. "You all right?"

No. "Yeah, I'm tight. What's up?"

"Swole talked to Cecilia Groves."

"Already? That was fast."

"I guess Cecilia attends a weekly yoga class at the fitness center, so Swole conveniently ran into her today. Anyway, she has given us permission to search the property."

SIXTEEN

BLADE

I'd never known a more infuriatingly unreasonable woman in my whole life.

To say that Kat's reaction was unexpected would be an understatement. It had never occurred to me to mention that I was a prospect for Outlaw Souls, and her attitude toward the club was baffling.

Clearly, she'd been fed a line of bullshit about us and wasn't willing to listen to reason.

Fine, I told myself. *Her loss.*

I spent the day stewing over the argument we'd had this morning and trying to ignore the tension in the air. I kept my curtain pulled around my work station all day, and she did the same. The atmosphere of the shop had changed so quickly.

I skipped lunch since I was in the middle of a tattoo on a woman's lower back around noon, so I was starving by the time I left the shop at the end of the night. I hopped on my bike while Kat and Piper walked across the parking lot to their cars and Brie locked up the building. I was the first one out of the parking lot, and I headed straight to Tiny's diner.

"Okay, maybe it's time to calm down," Piper said.

"At the time, I thought I knew who I was sleeping with," I bit out, ignoring her. "You guys go out of your way to harass Las Balas, declaring war, and for what? To make yourselves feel like big men by pushing out the only other motorcycle club in La Playa?"

"Are you really this naive? You think that Las Balas are the good guys in this fight?"

"You know what? You're new to Outlaw Souls, so I'll give you some advice. Don't piss off your president. I've heard that he's got a violent history, and I'd hate for you to learn the hard way that you've misplaced your loyalty."

I crossed into my workspace and pulled the curtain shut around me before he could reply. I didn't want to see his face right now, I was too worked up. Taking a seat on my stool, I dug around in my purse until I found my last piece of gum. I popped it into my mouth as I heard Blade mumble something about crazy women before the telltale sound of metal against metal that was the track of the curtain signaled he'd closed the one around his station, as well.

"Well, today's going to be fun," Piper said, and I hated that she was in an awkward situation, but it wasn't my fault. Blade was the bad guy here, and it was a shame because I really liked him.

know about my ties to a rival club, but I couldn't help feeling betrayed. I thought he was a good guy, but how could I believe that after being told my whole life that Outlaw Souls were the enemy?

I wasn't naive enough to think Las Balas were all stand-up guys. I knew that they got up to trouble sometimes. So if *they* claimed that Outlaw Souls were bad people, the rival club must get up to some bad shit.

"How can you align yourself with those people?" Blade asked, and I narrowed my eyes at him.

"Me? Look who's talking. And I'll have you know that my father is a member and my brother's a prospect of Las Balas."

"So, is *everyone* in your family a piece of shit?"

"Whoa," Piper's voice distracted me from the tirade I was prepared to throw at Blade. "What's going on here?"

She'd just walked in, and I saw Brie lingering behind her, watching us with concerned eyes.

"You won't believe this," I told my best friend. "Blade's an Outlaw Soul now."

"What?" she looked to Blade, who nodded with a stubborn glint in his eye.

"I was initiated on Saturday." He shrugged out of his jacket and showed them both the patch on the back. I forced myself not to ogle his thick arm muscles that were easy to see through his tight shirt.

"Oh," Piper's eyes flitted to me for a second before widening. "Wow. That's...unfortunate."

That was one way to put it.

"I can't believe this," I sighed. "I slept with the enemy."

At this, a dark anger flashed in Blade's eyes, and there was a rough edge to his voice when he spoke. "You didn't complain at the time."

"You ever hear of a coincidence?"

"Okay." She raised her hands in defense. "I get it. None of my business."

When I walked into the back of the shop, Blade was already there, but Piper hadn't arrived yet. I watched him for a long moment as he stood with his back to me, a combination of confusion and denial keeping my feet rooted to the floor.

"What the hell is that?" I asked, my voice sharp.

Blade turned with his brow furrowed. "What? What's wrong?"

I'd seen Blade wear his leather jacket before, and I'd even ridden on the back of his bike, but there was no way he'd been wearing an Outlaw Souls patch before today.

"You can't seriously be an Outlaw Soul." It wasn't a question, because I didn't want him to confirm it.

"You have a problem with motorcycle clubs?"

"I have a problem with that one," I said, sitting the remaining three coffees down on the counter and crossing my arms over my chest.

"Why?"

He seemed genuinely curious, but beneath that, I could sense his loyalty to Outlaw Souls. I'd seen it in my father long enough to recognize it. I lifted my chin and met his gaze head-on.

"I'm connected to Las Balas," I said, not sure how else to phrase it. Mad Dog had said I was family, but I wasn't so sure about that. My dad and my brother, sure, but I was more like a close family friend. My dad and brother were definitely family.

Understanding seemed to dawn on Blade's face. "That doesn't mean anything."

"Be serious," I snapped angrily. I knew that Blade didn't

"Absolutely."

I had the feeling that he was waiting for me to extend this invitation. This whole time, I had assumed that he was okay because he had Lexie, that she was all support he needed, but now I wasn't so sure. Maybe I wasn't the only one feeling alone since our mom died.

I WAS in a good mood when I walked into work on Monday morning. I'd had a hell of a weekend, starting with great sex and ending with a big dose of personal growth. I walked into Ink Envy while holding a drink carrier with four coffees made to everyone's specifications. I enjoyed working closely with a small group of people like this. I'd been employed by large companies in the past while working in housekeeping or for restaurant franchises. Employees didn't matter to those businesses. Everyone was easily replaceable. We were just numbers on a page. I knew that Brie cared about us and that she saw us as talented individuals and friends.

"Good morning," I said as I sat her cappuccino on the counter in front of her.

"I just cleaned that glass, you know," she said, picking up the cup and taking a sip.

"You're welcome," I replied, and she smiled.

"You're chipper for a Monday morning," she commented. "Have a good weekend?"

There was a twinkle in her eye, and I wondered what she knew about it.

"Sure."

"Funny, Blade seems to be in a good mood, too. Makes me think it might be related."

I couldn't stand living in a house haunted by my memories of her anymore. It was making me miserable.

There was a knock on my front door, and I grabbed two of the bags for donation, dragging them with me down the hall. I was sweaty, and my messy hair was pulled into a bun at the top of my head, but I didn't care. I knew who was on the other side of the door, and I wasn't looking to impress him.

"What's this stuff?" Jason asked as I pulled open the door.

"It's why I texted you to come over. It's for Goodwill."

He reached down and took a bag, grunting with surprise at the weight.

"What the hell do you have in here?" he asked, heaving it over to Lexie's car, which I'd asked him to bring instead of his bike.

"Clothes, mostly."

"You mean..."

"Yeah," I nodded. "I cleaned out Mom's room."

When Jason came back up the porch steps, he threw an arm over my shoulders. "Good for you, sis."

"I'll admit, it feels better."

"Yeah, you can't keep a shrine to her in this house and still expect to be comfortable living here."

"I miss her."

"Me too," he said, giving my shoulders a squeeze. Jason let go and grabbed the second bag to put in his car. We weren't exactly the lovey-dovey type, so I wasn't expecting much more than his help. The hug was a bonus.

"Hey, do you want to get together next week for dinner?" I asked.

"On Sunday?"

"Yeah."

ries. I told myself that the weather was making me melancholy, but I knew better. Something needed to change.

Sundays are for family. Okay, Mom.

I walked to her room, my bare feet making the floor creak in the hall. When I went into her room this time, I forced myself to do something, anything productive. Grabbing the comforter in both hands, I yanked it off the bed, followed by the sheets. When the mattress was bare, I went to the window and took down the curtains, adding them to the pile on the floor.

It was crazy the way that these simple acts loosened a knot in the center of my chest that I hadn't even realized was there. It felt like a purge, and I was shocked that I wanted to keep going. Whipping open the closet, I pulled all the clothes off the hangers, not stopping until they were all bare. It wasn't until I turned and saw all the fabric piled up on the floor that I realized I was crying.

I hated that. Crying made me feel stupid and weak, but there was nothing to be done about it. This was long-overdue, and I had a feeling that I would never be able to get through it without tears. In the end, it might make me feel better to finally cry. I had refused to allow myself to do it before now.

I spent all afternoon in that room, emptying the dresser and pulling everything out from under the bed. I got rid of almost everything, bagging up the clothes to be donated and throwing away anything else that I didn't want to keep. By the end of the day, I was standing in the middle of a room with a bare bed and an empty dresser.

Nothing in here reminded me of my mom anymore, and I felt a twinge of guilt at the relief that gave me. I didn't want to forget her, which would be impossible, anyway, but ride would be miserable. Even with a helmet and jacket, he'd be soaked.

I brewed myself a cup of coffee while grabbing a container of leftover Chinese food from the fridge. I ate the chow mein cold while leaning against the kitchen counter, thinking about the way my mother and I would spend our Sundays when she was alive.

She'd found religion in the last five years of her life and always insisted on going to the church's early service. I knew she wanted me to go with her, but I'd never been interested, usually sleeping in until she got home. I regretted that now. Whether or not I wanted to listen to a sermon and sing songs, or whatever they did at her church, I should've gone just to spend that time with her. Because it was important to her.

I threw my empty takeout container into the trash, thinking about the big meals she always made after getting home from church. I'd help her with that, at least. She insisted that Sunday afternoons were a time for family, and home cooking was a big part of that. Jason and Lexie always came over, and the four of us would spend hours at the kitchen table. My mom would playfully tease Jason about giving her grandchildren, and I'd always promise to bring home a man with a big appetite sometime, even though we all knew I didn't do serious relationships often. It was just a part of our routine.

After my mom had died, Jason and Lexie tried to keep the tradition going, even offering to come over and cook the food with me, despite that Jason was terrible at it. But I couldn't do it. It wasn't the same without her, and it felt like a mockery.

I drank two cups of coffee while I was lost in my memo-

FIFTEEN
KAT

I woke up late on Sunday, past noon. I had slept like a rock, practically passing out as soon as I got out of the shower. Now, my hair was a matted mess from being wet when I fell asleep, and my body was achy from running around the crowded bar. I stretched and yawned as I got out of bed, snatching up my jeans where I'd shoved my tips into my pockets the night before. Sitting cross-legged on the bed, I counted out the bills, finding that I'd earned about six hundred dollars.

Not too bad for one night's work.

I pulled a shoebox off the top shelf in my closet and added the tip money to the cash already in there. I had over four-thousand dollars now, probably enough to buy a nice used bike. I smiled to myself. I would start shopping around for one this week.

I'd slept in a t-shirt and pair of panties, but now I pulled on a pair of pajama pants. I was sticking around the house today, so it didn't really matter what I wore. I might as well be comfortable. Going to the kitchen, I saw grey clouds through the window and thought of Blade. If it rained, his of us stayed to drink for a couple of hours, celebrating. When the party finally broke up around one-thirty, I rode home. For some reason, when I got there, I thought of Kat. The only thing that was missing from this evening was finishing it between her legs.

I stripped as I walked into the bedroom, tossing clothes around carelessly, and fell across the bed with no grace whatsoever. Pulling my phone out of my discarded pants at the foot of the bed, I fired off a quick text to her. I wanted her to know that I was thinking about her even though I wouldn't be available to see her tomorrow.

Just before I passed out for the night, I thought about this being the first time I ever wanted to share good news with a woman. Kat was definitely going to be the first person to ride on the back of my bike now that I was an Outlaw Soul.

"Now, we have one other piece of business to discuss," Ryder said. "Blade, come up here."

I did, trying to hide my confusion.

"I think it's time that we vote on adding another patch to our ranks."

Holy shit.

"Blade has proved himself to be loyal to this club. Trainer, as his sponsor, do you approve?"

"I do."

"Then, we vote. All in favor?"

Once again, everyone approved. I felt the unmistakable feeling of something significant sliding into place for me. I was a Patch, an Outlaw Soul. These were my brothers and sisters now.

"Motion passed," Ryder clapped me on the back. "Welcome to the club."

Everyone raised their beers before drinking in unison. It was their way of welcoming me, and I grinned. This was my future. I took the jacket that Trainer pulled out of a duffle bag that I hadn't noticed was sitting in the chair beside him and pulled it on. It was a perfect fit, and my chest swelled with pride knowing that the Outlaw Souls patch was displayed on the back.

The meeting broke up soon after that, with Trainer, our Road Captain, planning out a ride for us all to take tomorrow afternoon. Apparently, it was tradition when a new member was voted in. I could see the jealousy in Axel's face when the meeting broke up and I came outside to tell him the news, but I knew he'd get over it. It sucked to be the only Prospect, but I was sure he'd be voted in soon enough. Outlaw Souls were good about rewarding people that paid their dues.

I was flying high for the rest of the evening, and a group

"I'm betting they're buried," Trainer said. "That's what I would've done."

"Agreed," Hawk chimed in. "I checked out the property that Luca's been showing interest in. There's a small amount of wooded area on the property, but probably not enough to hide a building or anything. The only place he could have put it is in the earth. A metal detector would do the job of finding the stash."

"Sure, but then we run into the same problem Luca's having," Ryder said. "We can't be seen messing around on a random piece of land without permission. The last thing we need is to draw attention from the cops."

"I'll talk to Cecilia," Swole offered. "She knows that we've got her back. I'm sure she'll give us access."

"Good. Then, we find the weapons and make a deal with Luca."

"Wait a minute," Chalupa said from the back. "We're probably talking about big money here if the mob is going to so much trouble to find these weapons."

"Yeah, but no amount is worth going to war with the damn mob," Hawk pointed out. "I say we get rid of the shit."

"Agreed," Ryder nodded. "I move that we vote."

"Seconded," Swole said.

"All in favor?"

There was a chorus of "Aye," as everyone except me voted. I didn't have voting rights yet.

"Motion passed," Ryder announced. "Swole, you talk to Cecilia, and Hawk, you get as many metal detectors as you can get your hands on. The sooner we get this shit taken care of, the better."

I sat down, happy with the way this went. I'd proved myself by providing useful information, which was exactly what I'd set out to do. I wanted to pull my weight here.

Groves. The question is why." Ryder nodded in my direction, which I took as my cue to speak.

I stood at my seat, leaning my ass against the edge of the table as I turned to address everyone.

"So, Luca runs the street fighting ring I've been wrapped up in," I started. "I didn't know him well at first, but it turns out that he's a grade-A weirdo."

There were chuckles, but I didn't pause. "He also works for a big-time arms dealer."

"You sure about that?" Hawk asked, his eyes sharp.

"Yeah, and I got the impression it's all connected to the mob. Raymond Groves was wrapped up with them, too. That's why he was killed. Luca was sent to La Playa to find out where Raymond stashed a bunch of weapons that belong to them."

"Shit," Trainer muttered, shaking his head.

"Yeah," Ryder said. "That's the kind of trouble that we don't need here."

"Well, it's already here. Luca wants me to put pressure on the widow to give him the land where the weapons are hidden."

"Why? Seems like a lot of trouble for him to go to." Ryder said.

"He's not as stupid as he looks. He's not willing to draw attention to the area or himself by fucking around there without permission."

"And you told him you would?"

"What choice did I have?"

"Well, that accelerates our timeline," Swole said, looking concerned. "We can't have him getting wise to our boy's deception."

"Agreed," Ryder said. "We need to find those damn guns and get Luca out of La Playa."

FOURTEEN
BLADE

I walked into the back room at the Blue Dog, surprised by how different it looked when it was full of people. Most of the club had already arrived, and I got a few surprised looks as I took a seat next to Ryder, but no one said anything.

Chels, the only full-time bartender at the Blue Dog, came in with buckets full of ice and bottles of beer. She placed one on each table, and we helped ourselves. The feeling of brotherhood here was evident in the relaxed atmosphere and the small talk that filled the room while we waited. I'd been told that the meetings weren't always fully attended under the last president, but since Ryder took over a few years ago, nearly everyone showed up.

"Okay, let's get started," Ryder said when all the members had arrived. He stood in front of the room with his hand in his pockets. "This meeting was called for one reason. To discuss Luca Bianchi."

There was murmuring around the room, and I heard someone behind me mutter, "Asshole."

"Yeah, we all know what's up. He offed Raymond

"You reek of stale beer," I complained, turning in the direction of his apartment.

"And you think you don't?"

He chuckled, and I found myself smiling despite myself.

"Give me a break. I had to deal with assholes all night."

"Yeah," he sighed, scrubbing a hand down his face. "I know Snake's an asshole, but he's all talk."

"Well, maybe someone should shut him up."

I could hear the bitterness in my own voice, but I didn't care. I couldn't pretend that he hadn't hurt my feelings with his indifference.

"Yeah, maybe someone should," he replied vaguely, turning to look out the window. I clamped down on my disappointment. Mad Dog could call me a part of the family all he wanted, but that didn't matter. My dad put the club members first.

I pulled up in front of the shitty apartment he lived in, feeling uneasy being on this street at this time of night. It was a rough neighborhood, and hanging out in the open was just asking for trouble. I wasn't worried about my dad, though. He'd lived here for ten years. This definitely wasn't the first time he'd stumbled home trashed in the middle of the night.

"Thanks for the ride, Katherine," he said as he got out of the car.

He was the only one that called me that. Ever since I was a little girl, he'd used my full name. It was something that always gave me a wave of affection for the man, even when it made me feel stupid.

"Goodnight, Dad," I replied just before he shut the door. I drove away the second he was inside the building, ready for some sleep.

The next few hours were uneventful, and when last call arrived at three, I had a pocket full of bills and was ready to get off my feet. I fired off a text to Jason, letting him know that he owed me big-time, and headed out the door.

I waited until I was in my car to check my phone, which had been tucked into my back pocket for most of the night. I had two text messages. One from Jason, agreeing that he did owe me a big one for covering for him. The second one was from Blade, and I smiled to myself as I sat there reading it.

Thinking of you tonight, Kitten. I have plans with friends tomorrow. But see you at work Monday.

I typed out a quick response, even though it was late and he'd likely be asleep already.

Thinking of you too. I'll bring the coffee Monday.

Tacking on a winky face, I pressed send before starting my car. I had nothing planned for tomorrow, so I would probably sleep in and spend the day in my pajamas. This half-formed plan was pushed out of my tired mind when I was about to exit the parking lot. My eyes landed on my dad, stumbling toward his motorcycle.

Oh, hell no.

Changing direction, I pulled up alongside him and rolled down the passenger window.

"Get in," I said when he blinked at me.

"Nah," he shook his head. "I'm good."

"No, you're really not, and I'm too tired for this shit," I snapped impatiently. I was already pissed at him, and now he was wasting my time. "Get. In. The. Car."

"Fine," he mumbled. "Don't get your panties in a bunch."

He opened the passenger door and got into the seat. I crinkled my nose.

jerking his head toward the door. They surged forward, taking hold of the man by the arms and pulling him out the door, ignoring his protests about having opened a tab. A woman shot out of her seat near the door.

"Luke!" she cried out, pushing her way through the crowd to follow.

"No, don't go after him," I called out, starting to make my way to the edge of the bar to stop her. Mad Dog blocked my path. "He tried to roofie her," I told him angrily.

"Not our problem. You stopped him, and I kicked him out. If she wants to follow a guy like that around, she's a pathetic lost cause, anyway."

"It's not her fault that he's a dick," I argued, but the woman was already out the door.

"And it's not our business. Las Balas worry about ourselves instead of interfering with others."

"I'm not La Balas."

He shrugged, looking over at my dad, who was in the middle of hitting on some woman in a tube top. "Maybe not, but you're family. Consider yourself lucky in that."

I wasn't sure what to think about that. I knew that the club was probably involved in things that I didn't want to know about, and some of its members could be pretty rough around the edges, but Mad Dog was right. I'd always been family because my dad was a member.

"Now," Mad Dog turned to Winger. "Was that true about his opening a tab? You have his debit card?"

"Yeah," Winger said.

"Then, the next round's on him!" Mad Dog shouted, and the bar went wild. We were slammed after that, and I even treated myself to a shot of tequila from the guy. I probably should have felt guilty about that, but I figured anyone that called me a bitch owed me a drink.

gum from my purse before walking back out and resuming my position behind the bar.

"I'm not going back over there," I told Winger firmly. He frowned, but I didn't care. I wasn't trying to join the club—not that they accepted women as members—so it didn't matter if I made a good impression, anyway.

Winger had just finished making two drinks, a draft of beer, and a screwdriver, and handed them over to the customer that was waiting. As the guy picked up the drink, I saw that he dropped a small white tablet into the screwdriver, which dissolved almost immediately.

"No fucking way," I snapped, turning away from Winger to grab the screwdriver out of the man's hand. He resisted, and the fruity drink ended up spilling all over the bar between us, also splashing my shirt and his.

"You stupid bitch," he snarled, but I wasn't going to back down. The guy wasn't a member of Las Balas, so I didn't have to worry about going up against the whole club. Besides, I hoped that the club would never allow a member to do such a thing, not that I'd ever seen the rule book. It was strictly off-limits to non-members.

"Out," I said, pointing to the door. I could feel the eyes of the people around me, staring at us. "You won't be served here. So, leave now."

The man scoffed. "Who the hell are you to kick me out? Just some whore bartender."

"That's enough," said a voice from behind the jerk that was staring daggers at me. He turned, and I saw the president of Las Balas, Mad Dog Diaz, standing there. I didn't know if the man recognized him as the president of the club or if he simply picked up on the heavy aggression emanating from Mad Dog, but either way, he shrank back. Mad Dog made eye contact with two Las Balas patches nearby, unloading it and gathering the empties to take away and be cleaned.

"Thanks, Kitty-Kat." The man speaking to me was Snake, a man my father's age who I had known most of my life. He was eyeing me like I was a piece of meat, and I felt my skin crawl. I knew damn well that he had a wife at home.

"You're welcome," I said through tight lips.

"Don't be a downer, Katherine," my dad chimed in, and I could see that the alcohol was starting to affect him. His words were slightly slurring, and the whites around his eyes were red.

"Yeah, Kitty-Kat," Snake said, and I couldn't help comparing his creepy nickname to the way that Blade called me Kitten. No comparison. "Give us a smile."

I wouldn't. Maybe it would encourage them to tip me, but his demand annoyed me too much to comply.

"Winger will be back with more beer when you need it," I said to the table at large, refusing to address Snake directly.

As I turned and started to walk away, my tray now loaded up with their empty pitchers. I had only walked one step when I heard Snake speak again. This time he was addressing my father.

"That daughter of yours is a real stuck up bitch."

I froze, anger coursing through me as I waited to hear how my dad would respond. Instead of the righteous indignation I expected, he simply chuckled.

Stupid, irritating tears threatened to make an appearance, but I blinked a few times, willing them away. Going back into the tiny kitchen behind the bar, I put the pitchers into a rack with a bunch of glasses that needed to be cleaned and ran it all through the dishwasher. I grabbed a stick of as the enemy. They were vindictive and out to hurt Las Balas at every turn.

"Here you go, ladies," I said, handing over the drinks I made. I took their money, pocketing my tip. Jason was right about that. I was making a good amount in tips.

I turned around just as Winger shoved a tray with two pitchers of beer into my hands. I looked at him questioningly as I struggled to balance the heavy drinks.

"It's your turn," he explained, nodding to the table where my dad sat. I sighed. This was probably the rowdiest bunch of people in the bar, and I had to navigate through the room to get there.

Holding the tray high, I weaved around groups of people dancing and tables where customers were talking loudly to each other, even though the band wasn't currently playing. I had almost reached the table when a large hand reached out and grabbed my ass. I jolted, almost sending the tray flying, but I was able to steady myself just in time. Looking over my shoulder, I glared at the man with his hand on me.

"If you don't take your damn hand off of me, you're gonna get a pitcher of beer over your head."

He pulled his hand away while I glared, but didn't look apologetic at all. *Asshole.*

When I turned back around, I saw that the men at my dad's table had seen the whole thing and were laughing their asses off. I scowled. Why couldn't my dad care enough to be pissed when a man put his hands on me?

Maybe that wasn't fair. I could handle myself, after all, and the guy hadn't pushed it further. Surely, my dad would have done something if he had. I hoped.

I closed the distance to the table and set the tray down,

parent. I didn't like it, but I suspected that a part of me would always wish that I had a better relationship with him. I thought that might be the reason that Jason was trying to join Las Balas in the first place, and it made me sad for him.

As the band took a break, I turned my attention back to the line of people pressed up against the bar, trying to get my attention. A group of women that were young—maybe too young to be in here, but this wasn't the kind of place that carded—crowded around one end of the bar together and ordered five mixed drinks. I took that one since Winger was more suited to slinging beers and pouring shots. While shaking up a cocktail, I caught snippets of a conversation between two club members sitting at the bar.

"We need to figure out something big before we start losing members and assets."

"It's not easy. We've lost too much damn money in the last two years."

"It's the damn Outlaw Souls. They're always up in our business, and it hurts our bottom line."

I shook my head at the mention of the other motorcycle club. I wasn't sure what these two men were talking about, but it couldn't be anything good. I'd heard stories about the Outlaw Souls and how seriously they took the rivalry between the clubs. Apparently, they didn't think La Playa was big enough for more than one motorcycle club. There were even rumors that the Outlaw Souls were responsible for the last bar owned by Las Balas burning down in the middle of the night. Nothing had been confirmed, but I knew my dad believed it. Others said it was an insurance scheme pulled off by the president of the club.

I didn't know what was true as far as that went, but I knew that every member of Las Balas saw the Outlaw Souls

Balas alongside my brother and seemed like a cool guy. At least he didn't hit on me.

"Yeah, I'm pretty sure we've exceeded max capacity here," I agreed.

All the seats were taken, leaving only standing room. There was a space in front of the stage for a dance floor, and as I watched, a large group of women crowded the front, forming a mosh pit in front of the band while others danced. That seemed like a bad idea to me, but I had no doubt that the Las Balas enforcer could handle a brawl between a bunch of women if it came to that.

It was the burly men that concerned me.

But for now, everything seemed mostly calm. My eyes strayed to a table in the corner where my dad was sitting. I hadn't seen him in a couple of weeks, and he'd looked mildly surprised when I showed up tonight but didn't go out of his way to greet me. He just gave me a smile and a wave before joining the president of the club and a handful of other members in draining the three pitchers of beer that we were told to keep supplied at the table at all times.

I watched as he took a big swig from his glass, wiping the foam out of his mustache with the sleeve of his shirt. He'd always sported a full beard and mustache, and I didn't think I'd even recognize him without it.

I had mixed emotions every time I saw my dad here, among his fellow club members. This was where he spent all his time when I was growing up and my mom was trying to raise two kids on her own. I'd barely known him back then, and now it felt more like we were acquaintances more than anything else.

So, why did I want his acknowledgment? Why did it bother me that he didn't at least come over and say hi?

I chalked it up to a biological need for affection from a

THIRTEEN

KAT

The Pit was packed. The band they'd booked was good, playing hard rock covers at a nearly deafening volume. I had been there an hour and was already regretting my choice of a V-neck top since I had to keep leaning over the bar to hear the drink orders. Since there were twice as many men as women in the bar, I found that most of the customer's eyes trailed down to my cleavage when I did this.

"When's your break, gorgeous?" A guy with a teardrop tattoo under his eye asked. He was the third one to try this.

"Sorry, buddy," I said, handing over a beer and shot of whiskey. "No rest for the wicked."

He looked annoyed as he took the drinks and stepped away from the bar, but I paid him no mind, just moved on to the next guy waiting to place his order.

Every Las Balas member that I'd ever met was in the bar tonight, but that was no surprise. I could smell pot in the air, but couldn't spot the source in this crowd.

"Good thing Las Balas has paid off the fire marshall," Winger said from beside me. He was a Prospect for Las to make sure there was no leak around the drain plug as the fresh oil worked through the system.

"Hey, you got a minute?" Ryder asked.

"Sure," I said, wiping my hands off on a rag. "You want to talk about Luca?"

"We'll cover that later, at the meeting."

"I'm attending the meeting?" I asked with mild surprise. Prospects didn't have voting rights, so they didn't attend the meetings. You had to be a Patch for that.

"Yes. We all need to hear what you have to say."

"Then, what's up?"

"I hear you're working at Ink Envy."

"Yeah, you been there?"

He shook his head. "No, but I'm looking to get some work done. You up for it?"

"Sure. What did you have in mind?"

"On my forearm," he held it out, showing me the unmarked skin. "I want a skull with the stem of a red rose between its teeth."

"Sounds badass."

"I saw a similar picture a few days ago and have been thinking about it ever since. Can you do it?"

"Definitely. Tuesday afternoon?"

"I'll be there."

I left the garage after that. I had a few hours to kill before the club meeting, so I decided to go for a solo ride. Laying on the throttle on the straight-aways so that I felt like I was flying down the road and weaving through the curves on the backroads that got so intense my knees damn near touched the ground, it was a perfect afternoon. The best thing about riding was the thrill of it, and I liked to push it sometimes.

You only live once, and I wasn't going to waste it.

"Do you want to come to lunch with us, Blade?" Eve asked, pulling me out of my thoughts and back to the present. I shook my head to clear it. "We're going to Tiny's."

"Thanks for the invitation, but I've got to finish this oil change."

She nodded with understanding.

"I'll see you at the meeting later," Trainer said as he polished off his beer and tossed the empty bottle into the trash.

I went back to changing my oil, finishing the job quickly. I was alone in the garage now, but I knew that someone was probably back in the office. As one of Outlaw Souls properties, it was a potential target for our rival motorcycle club, Las Balas, so it was never left unattended.

Las Balas were trouble. They dabbled in all sorts of shady shit, and Outlaw Souls had made it their mission to stop some of the more nefarious activities. Before I became a prospect with Outlaw Souls, they had busted up a sex trafficking ring run by Las Balas. They were kidnapping young women from La Playa and the surrounding areas to force into sex work or even sell as sex slaves. It was some nasty business involving several of the higher-up members of Las Balas. Since then, there had been a few incidents involving drug dealing and car theft.

Outlaw Souls weren't saints, and they didn't pretend to be. But as far as outlaw motorcycle clubs went, they were among the good ones. They worked to clean up La Playa, which was why I was eager to join the club. It was the reason I had gone out of my way to figure out what Luca was up to.

Ryder came out of the back office as I was disposing of the old oil I'd drained out of my bike. The bike was running, boy came running in, glasses askew. Dominic was Trainer's stepson, but he treated the boy like he was his own.

"Dad, you won't believe what happened today," Dominic said excitedly as he came to Trainer's side.

Trainer's face softened as he looked at his kid. "Tell me about it."

While Dominic talked to Trainer about the new friend he'd made and the school play that he wanted to audition for, I saw two other people enter the garage. Trainer's wife, Eve, came into the garage carrying a baby girl in her arms.

She greeted me with a smile before pecking Trainer on the lips. I found myself staring at a perfect little family. My focus was on the way that Eve and Trainer looked at each other. There was so much love there that I could practically see it in the air between them.

The twinge of jealousy I felt surprised me. I'd never concerned myself with the idea of settling down. I'd always thought that the idea of finding someone to be with forever was unrealistic, but that might have been because I didn't understand my parent's relationship. How could two people who were so different spend their lives together? I always suspected that it was because they'd gotten pregnant with my older brother early in the relationship, and marriage had seemed like the best option at the time. But now that I was around happy couples regularly with so many of the Outlaw Souls being in happy relationships, I found that I wanted that happiness.

No kids, though. Trainer's children were great, and I genuinely enjoyed being around them and others, but I didn't want to raise one myself. It just wasn't something I was interested in. I preferred the idea of sharing my life with one other person, a woman who didn't want children either.

thing. When I arrived at the garage, Trainer was there, working on one of his bikes.

I pulled into the bay next to him, greeting him with a nod. He was busy mounting a tire, so I didn't strike up a conversation. We couldn't really talk over the blaring rap music, anyway. I got to work on my oil change, letting my mind drift to the night before. My cock twitched in my pants at the memory of Kat's naked body illuminated in the low light of her bedroom.

I was so lost in my memory that I wasn't paying attention to what was going on around me until Trainer turned down the music until I could barely hear it. I stood from where I'd been crouched beside my bike for the last ten minutes.

"You want a beer?" he asked.

"Hell, yeah."

Trainer walked over to a mini-fridge against the wall and pulled out two bottles. Using the edge of the counter to pop the tops of the bottles, he handed one to me and leaned against the bike he was working on. It was a nice little Harley with a burnt orange paint job.

"You like it?" He asked, running a hand over the tank. "Still needs a valve adjustment, and I ordered a windshield that should arrive in two weeks."

"She's a beaut," I said. It was low to the ground, which was good for riders that were shorter.

"It's small for me, but I like it, too. I don't think I'll have a problem finding a buyer when she's ready."

"She?"

"Oh, yeah," Trainer smiled. "All motorcycles are female."

"Good to know," I smiled.

The door of the auto shop opened, and a nine-year-old

TWELVE
BLADE

After leaving Kat's house, I went home and changed my clothes. The shower I took this morning was refreshing and good for washing away the semen and sweat that lingered on my skin from the night before, but putting on my dirty clothes afterward made my skin crawl.

It was worth it to have spent the night with Kat. She was wild in bed, taking what she wanted from me in a way that drove me crazy. Afterward, she had fallen asleep quickly, but I lay in the darkness, listening to her heavy breathing and running my fingers through her hair.

I had slept with a lot of women over the years. I didn't think of myself as a player, but it was a term that had been hurled at me a time or two from women that took it hard when I didn't develop feelings for them.

Things with Kat felt deeper. I wasn't sure how far our connection could go, but for the first time, I was interested in exploring such a thing. *Could she tame me?*

I rode my bike to Ortega Auto for an oil change. It was almost due for one, and I liked to stay on top of that kind of out to see that the mirrors had fogged up. To my surprise, there was a message written on the glass for me.

Have a good day, Kitten.

I smiled. After that message, I had a feeling that I would.

well that she was gone. It was just easier on my heart to avoid the topic.

"That's okay. I have to go change my oil in the bike today and meet up with some friends later." He stood, rinsing his bowl in the sink. "I'll get dressed."

He walked to my bedroom while I stayed at the kitchen island, but after a moment, I got up and followed him. He'd already put his jeans on and was pulling his shirt over his head when I walked in.

"I miss her," I blurted. Blade paused, looking at me in confusion. I clarified, "My mom. I miss her every day. Haven't even been able to clean out her room yet."

Blade closed the distance between us until we were close enough to touch. "You don't have to talk about it. I get it. Trust me."

Leaning forward, I rested my cheek against his chest, and he wrapped his arms around me. Neither of us spoke for a moment.

"I really do need to go," he finally said. "Should I wait until you're out of the shower to take you to get your car?"

I shook my head. "Don't worry about it. Jason can take me later. He owes me."

"I'll call you, okay?"

"You better."

As Blade left, I couldn't help feeling the loneliness of the house once again.

Maybe I should get a roommate.

Stepping into the shower, I cranked it over to the hottest temperature I could stand and just stood under it for several minutes, letting the heat loosen up my sore muscles. I had to fill in for Jason at The Pit tonight, so I needed to be at the top of my game.

When I was done with my shower routine, I stepped

There were two hands reaching for a white dove that was just out of reach. Underneath it, the words *until we meet again* were scrawled as well as the name and date. The date was twelve years ago, probably from when Blade was a teenager. I wanted to ask him who Mark was, but when he turned around, I noticed how relaxed he was. He seemed happy in this moment, and I didn't want to bring up a subject that was undoubtedly painful.

I decided to stop being stupid about my feelings for him, though. I liked the guy, and I just wasn't used to that.

We sat at my kitchen island together, each with a bowl of Cinnamon Toast Crunch in front of us. Not exactly the healthiest breakfast in the world, but it got the job done.

"Do you live here alone?" he asked, and I knew it was silly to be surprised by the question. The house was really too big for one person, so it made sense that he'd want to know. Still, I didn't like to talk about it.

"Yeah. My mom used to live here too, but she...uh, she doesn't anymore." I didn't say she was dead and gone forever, but Blade must have read the expression on my face because he reached out and took my hand in his.

"How long ago did it happen?"

I swallowed hard. Damn it. I hadn't intended to have a heavy conversation over breakfast.

"A little more than six months ago."

"I'm sorry." He gave my fingers a squeeze, and I allowed myself to have one moment where I accepted the comfort he was providing. Then, I pulled my hand away.

"I better get in the shower," I explained, but that wasn't the whole truth.

I was afraid to talk too much about it, scared of the reality of the situation becoming unavoidable. I wasn't having the easiest time accepting it, even though I knew full feeling. By the time I was done in there, the shower was off in my bathroom. I headed to the kitchen and started a pot of coffee.

When Blade walked into the room with just a towel around his waist, I felt my mouth go dry. I had gotten an idea of how well-built he was last night when we were in bed, but it was different to see his bare chest and abs in the light of day. Sinewy muscle covered his upper body, and the deep grooves of his six-pack were drool-worthy.

There were also dozens of tattoos. There were black tribal style tattoos banded around each of his biceps, a skull, a motorcycle, and a word written in another language. That was just what I could see on the front of his body.

My fingers itched with the urge to trace the lines of ink, to explore closer and discover what was hidden under, but I figured that would lead to more sex, and we should probably have breakfast first. Blade came to my side and pressed a chaste kiss against my cheek.

"Good morning, beautiful," he said. Stepping around me, he went for the coffee, and I was struck by how domestic it all was. When was the last time I'd had a man stay the night?

I couldn't even remember.

But this felt natural in a way that was unnerving. I liked Blade, and he was hotter than a lightning strike in bed, but I didn't expect to feel this comfortable with him in my space so quickly. It sort of freaked me out.

"Got any cereal?" he asked, sipping his black coffee.

At least he didn't expect me to cook him breakfast. I wasn't exactly a Susie Homemaker.

"In the cabinet behind you," I said, pointing.

When he turned to open the cabinet, I caught sight of a tattoo on his shoulder that was an unmistakable memorial.

I felt more than heard him chuckle lightly. He moved around for a moment, and I heard him toss the condom in the trash can I kept beside the bed. He pulled my comforter over the two of us while I struggled to stay awake. Then, I felt him kiss my forehead, and that unfamiliar feeling returned. It was a warm wave of affection, one that I'd never felt for a man before. It scared me, but I couldn't summon the energy to contemplate what it meant. I lost my battle with the Sandman and surrendered to sleep.

I AWOKE to the sound of the shower running the next morning. As someone that lived alone, I was confused at first. Then the night before came back to me, and I found myself sitting up in bed with a goofy smile on my face.

I stretched, mildly enjoying the slight soreness between my legs. It was evidence of the mind-blowing sex I'd enjoyed the night before.

I got out of bed, pulling on my robe as I went. The idea of joining Blade in the shower was appealing, but I decided against it. I needed to pee, and we weren't at a point in our relationship that I was comfortable doing so in the same room as him, even if he was enclosed in the shower stall. So, I went down the hall to the bathroom attached to the master suite, formerly my mom's. After relieving myself, I looked in the mirror while washing my hands and cringed. I didn't usually wear much make-up, but I'd dolled myself up a bit yesterday for the date. Now I looked like a raccoon where the eyeliner and mascara had smeared while I slept.

Yikes.

I took my time cleaning off every trace of make-up, splashing cold water on my face and enjoying the refreshing moan. I continued with that motion, over and over, until I settled into a rhythm.

"God, you're so deep," I said, cupping my own breasts.

My belly quivered as Blade rocked his hips under me, urging me to go faster. His hands took hold of my hips, and my breathing turned ragged as he moved me, lifting me up and ramming me down hard.

I knew he'd like it rough.

Every nerve ending in my body came to life, and I felt myself climbing higher and higher, closer to a climax. My thoughts were a jumbled mess, and the noises spilling from my mouth were unintelligible. It didn't matter. All that mattered were the sensations spreading throughout my whole body.

"Kat...I need you to come, baby. Do it for me," he ground out between clenched teeth. "Milk my cock, baby."

His dirty words pushed me over the edge. I felt like an explosion went off as an orgasm rocked my body. I could feel myself tightening around Blade's cock, and he barked out my name as he reached his own climax.

Time stood still as we both tried to catch our breath. I felt weak, my arms and legs shaky, but I didn't care. This was everything I wanted it to be, rough and utterly satisfying.

When I finally shifted and laid on the bed beside him, Blade pulled me close so that my head rested on his shoulder. His fingers ran through my hair, and I closed my eyes, enjoying the feeling. I was suddenly exhausted.

"You're fucking amazing, you know that?" Blade's voice was soft in the darkness, and I didn't think I'd ever heard him sound so sincere.

"You're not too bad yourself," I said, trying and failing to suppress a yawn.

"Take off your pants," I demanded, feeling powerful as I took charge.

He didn't comply immediately, as he watched me strip with wide eyes. I'd never seen someone look at me the way that he did—with reverence—and it made an unfamiliar emotion swell within my chest. I didn't know what to do with that, so I pushed it aside and focused on what my body was feeling.

I pulled open the drawer of my nightstand and grabbed a condom, and Blade finally took off his pants, kicking them onto the floor and laying flat as I crawled onto the bed beside him. His thick length stood up, and I didn't hesitate to take it in my hand. Blade was hard and hot and...oh God, *so big*.

I stroked him slowly, watching his face as he narrowed his eyes and let his breath out in a slow hiss. His soft skin glided over the stiff core, and I wondered what it tasted like.

But that would have to wait for another time. I couldn't deny myself the pleasure I'd been craving for another minute. I slid the condom onto his cock. He was watching my every move with hooded eyes, his hands fisted in the sheets on either side of his body.

"Ride me, Kitten," he said, and I positioned myself over him.

My eyes held his, which looked black in the darkness of the room, as I lowered myself onto his erection. My breath left me in a rush as I was stretched wide and pure pleasure radiated through me.

"*Fuck*," Blade cursed, and the look on his face was an expression of ecstasy.

Leaning forward, I lifted my hips until only the tip of his cock remained inside. Then, I took his entire length inside again in one swift movement, making both of us pressed against my own, the smooth warmth of his skin driving me wild.

My blood was pounding in my ears, and the only thing I could think about was getting the rest of our clothing off. I needed him inside of me like I'd never needed anything before.

"Blade," I gasped as his rock-hard erection rubbed at me through our clothing, hitting my sensitive clit. "Please."

I couldn't find the words to ask for what I wanted, but I didn't have to. Blade was in tune with my body, and it seemed that he was more than willing to give me what I needed.

Shoving a hand down the front of my jeans, he slipped his fingers past the waistband of my panties. When he reached my entrance, he let out a tortured moan.

"Fuck, Kitten. You're *soaking* for me."

His finger slid inside, and I thrust my hips up. Heat rolled through my body, and I bit my lip. God, it felt so good, but it wasn't enough.

"You like that, huh?" He asked, slipping another finger inside. I could feel myself clench around his digits and a needy moan left my lips. "You like the way I touch you?"

"Yes, Blade." I hardly recognized my own voice, it was so husky. "God, yes."

His mouth went back to my nipple as he pumped his fingers in and out faster. I knew what he was doing, working me up like this. He wanted to make me come, but I wasn't having any of that. I wanted to orgasm with him inside of me.

In a quick motion, I pushed against his shoulder, sending him onto his back. He let out a surprised grunt as his hand slid out of my pants. I shot him a flirty smile as I stood, unbuttoning my pants.

No words were needed as he followed me up to the front door of the house. I'd barely gotten the key turned in the lock when he was pulling me into his arms.

We stumbled across the threshold, a tangle of limbs as our tongues wrestled. Blade lifted me up so that my legs wrapped around his waist. His large hands held onto my ass as he blindly walked us into the living room, kicking the front door shut behind him.

I broke our kiss long enough to direct him to my bedroom while Blade's lips skimmed down my neck, making a shiver run down my spine when he sucked lightly at the juncture where my neck met my shoulder.

The curtains in my room were open, allowing a faint glow from the streetlight outside to illuminate the space just enough to see. I reached down to the hem of my shirt, ripping it off over my head and tossing it carelessly aside. Then, I reached back and popped open my bra clasp. As soon as it was out of the way, Blade let out a low growl and dropped me onto the bed, coming down on top of me and burying his face in my chest. I thrust my fingers into his short hair, holding him tight to me.

Blades tongue worked magic on my sensitive buds, making me arch my back and release a breathy moan. Grabbing hold of the back of his shirt, I fisted my fingers in it and pulled it over his head. I could see that his body was covered in tattoos, but it was too dark to make out the details. I'd have to check out the work later.

I needed more of him. Blade seemed to sense my desperate hunger and released my nipple. It came out of his mouth with a faint popping sound, and the cool air in the room made the wet tip almost painfully hard. He moved back to my mouth, grinding into me. His bare chest was

ELEVEN
KAT

Playing laser tag with Blade was a blast. I was pretty sure it was the most fun I'd ever had on a date. He won in the end, but I put up a hell of a fight. After an hour of running, ducking, and diving in the laser tag course, I would have expected to be too exhausted to do much else tonight. But as I climbed onto the back of Blade's bike, I felt energized by my need for him.

He started to head back to the tattoo shop, to drop me off at my car, but I wanted to be alone with him now. To hell with the car, I could pick it up tomorrow. I tapped him on the shoulder to get his attention.

"Take me home instead," I shouted to be heard over the roar of the motorcycle's engine.

"You sure?" he asked.

"Yes, definitely."

I gave him directions to my house. It didn't take long to get there, but by the time we arrived, I was fighting the urge to squirm on the back of the bike. Knowing what was coming made my core ache.

Blade parked in my driveway and turned off the bike.

The countdown clock above our heads was set to one hour, and we heard the locks click before the attendant told us we could begin.

I surged forward, opening my door and stepping into blackness. I froze, waiting for my eyes to adjust as the heavy door I'd just entered through closed behind me. There was loud techno music playing, drowning out any other sound. I wouldn't be able to tell where Kat was by hearing her footsteps.

After a few seconds, my eyes adjusted enough to see that there was a long wall to my right, which must be separating Kat and me. I held the plastic gun with two hands and headed to the left, where there was another hallway. At the end of it, the room opened up, revealing a space illuminated by blacklight, and the walls practically glowing with the paint on them. It was a large space, filled with square objects that could be used to hide behind or get in the way as obstacles. I touched one and found it to be cushioned on all sides for safety. There were doorways all over the room, leading to a maze that connected them and would be a good place to ambush an opponent.

My adrenaline spiked, and I tried to decide my next move when the light in the center of my chest flashed red.

"What the fuck?"

Movement made me turn to my right, where I spotted Kat running away, clearly laughing her ass off. I had just started to follow her when she disappeared through a doorway. My light turned green again, and I smirked while I raised my gun. She got the first shot, but I was ready for her now, and I loved a good challenge.

It was on.

The pizza arrived, and we dug in. Kat was honest when she said she wasn't afraid to eat in front of a man. She put away even more of the pizza than I did, and I found myself trying to figure out where it all went.

"I've always had a fast metabolism," she said, answering my unasked question.

Damn, it was refreshing to be with a woman like her. I had the impression that she wasn't putting on airs at all. I was getting the real Kat here, through and through. No games.

She offered to pay for half of the meal, but I took care of it. I wasn't the most old-fashioned of men, but I believed that the person that initiated the date should cover the bill. Besides, I'd planned everything.

I bid John a quick goodbye, and we left the restaurant. It seemed silly to get back on the bike just to ride such a small distance, so I took hold of her hand as we walked across the parking lot, then the street. The building that housed the laser tag course was brick, painted black with no windows. I had never been here before, but I'd played the game in other places.

I'd called ahead to reserve a time slot for the two of us, so it took no time to check in and get into our vests. The lights on my chest and back were blue while Kat's were green. If we shot each other, the lights would flash red for a few seconds. We had an hour, and whoever got the most shots in on their opponent would be the winner.

I knew I'd made a good choice when I looked over at Kat just before we went into the course. We were both standing in front of doors about ten feet apart, which were our individual entrances to the course. She was smiling from ear-to-ear, and her body was practically humming with excitement. She was pumped up.

face. I was just about to ask her about it when my phone buzzed in my pocket. I didn't want to be rude, but as a prospect, it was important that I could be reached at all times. It was a message from Ryder telling me that there would be a meeting tomorrow night.

"Sorry, just a second," I said, typing out a quick affirmative that I would be there.

Those bikes aren't going to watch themselves.

"Anyway," I tried to recall where we were in the conversation. "I come here at least once a week, but I chose it tonight because of our after-dinner activity."

She shot me a heated gaze, and I knew what she had in mind. My cock, still half-erect from thoughts of getting her naked, gave a little twitch in my pants.

"Oh, yeah?" she asked. "And what activity do you have in mind?"

Leaning closer to her, I beckoned for her to do the same. She did until our faces were only inches apart. I wanted to claim her sweet mouth again, but instead, I turned my head and pointed to a black building across the street.

"Laser tag?" Kat asked, and I could hear the surprise and excitement in her voice.

"Yep." I sat back in my seat. "But I have to warn you, I'm pretty good. You might not stand a chance."

"I'm gonna wipe that smug grin off your face once and for all," she said, also leaning back. "I can't believe you're taking me to play laser tag."

"Why not? I told you it would be more fun than a movie."

"It's just that some people might consider it childish."

"And what's wrong with that?" I asked. "I think we should all be a little childish sometimes."

"I agree."

"Kat, this is John, the owner of the best pizza shop you've ever been in."

"Wow. Those are some big words." She turned to John. "Does the food live up to the hype?"

"I like to think so," he said with a humble look.

I gestured to a booth by the door, and Kat slid into the seat. The inside of the restaurant was exactly what you'd expect of a small pizza place. There were red vinyl seats at the booths and matching chairs at the tables placed in straight rows on the floor. The glass front of the building provided an uninspiring view of the parking lot, and there were close-up pictures of pizzas on the walls. What really set the place apart was the product. John's grandmother came over from Sicily sixty years ago, bringing the recipe with her. It was authentic and tasted amazing.

There were a few other customers already seated, enjoying the food. It was never overly crowded here, making it the best-kept secret in La Playa.

"What toppings do you like?" I asked.

She shrugged. "Usually, just pepperoni."

"A woman after my own heart," I said, adding a little drama by placing my hand over the left side of my chest. It earned me a small chuckle.

I went to the counter to place our order, and John got to work immediately. He made the food right there in front of the customers, showing off as he stretched the dough by tossing it into the air and catching it.

"So, you're a regular here?" Kat asked when I sat back down.

"I'm not much of a cook, so I have a few favorite places that I go to eat regularly. You ever heard of Tiny's?"

"I don't really go to that part of town often," she said.

An emotion that I couldn't decipher flashed across her

The evening was perfect for a ride. We were heading to the eastern part of town, so the sun was at our backs as it slowly made its way across the sky to set in a couple of hours. The air was almost always a little humid in this town, being so close to the ocean, but it wasn't overly so tonight. Cool wind rushed over us as the motorcycle picked up speed, and Kat rested her head against my back.

It didn't take long to reach our destination. I pulled into the parking lot in front of a strip mall. There was a line of businesses, ranging from a video game store to a bakery. I had my sights set on the pizza place right in the middle, so I parked in front of it.

When we got off the bike and pulled our helmets off, Kat shook out her hair. The wind had whipped it around during the ride, and it was a mess, but I thought that it looked like she'd just had wild sex. I felt my cock start to stir at the notion of that, and I stepped closer to her. I hadn't kissed her again since that first time in the back room of the shop, and I needed another taste.

Cupping her cheek, I tilted her head back, and she parted her lips for me. The kiss was gentler than last time, but I still felt a blast of arousal at the contact. I wanted to consume her, but she pulled away after a few seconds.

"Come on," she said. "I'm starving."

We walked into the familiar restaurant. I had been coming here since I moved to La Playa, and in my opinion, it had the best pizza in town.

"Blade, I didn't know you were coming in tonight," John, the owner of the place, greeted me from behind the counter as I walked through the door. He was always here, tossing pizza dough every day. His eyes landed on Kat beside me, and he grinned. "And you've brought a *friend*."

"You ready to go?" I asked her as Ink Envy closed. She was smoking hot tonight with her tight jeans and a black tank top. Her hair was down, the long black locks flowing down to the middle of her back in waves, and I noticed that she'd put on a little more makeup than usual. I appreciated the effort, but she was gorgeous, even without it.

"Yep," she said, pulling on a black leather jacket. "Where are you taking me."

"I'm not saying," I smirked.

"You're lucky I like surprises."

We exited the shop together, and I mounted my bike, straightening it as I raised the kickstand. Kat didn't have to be told what to do as she came over and climbed on behind me, swinging her leg up in a smooth motion that suggested she'd done this a hundred times. It reminded me of my first day of work.

"Hey, who was it that picked you up from work the day we met?"

It was risky to ask her about another man at the beginning of our first date, but I couldn't suppress my curiosity.

"What, Jason?" she laughed lightly as she pulled her helmet onto her head. "You weren't jealous, were you?"

I knew she was teasing, but I decided to be honest.

"Yes, I was."

Kat scooted herself closer to me until her toned thighs were stretched around mine, and she wrapped her arms around my waist. Her face was beside my ear when she spoke.

"He's my brother."

Thank fuck.

I started the bike, feeling the vibrations from the engine at the base of my spine. Kat's grip tightened around me when I took off, pulling out onto the street.

My head spun with all this new information.

"So, you up for it?" Luca asked, and I had trouble figuring out what his question was referring to.

"Up for what?"

"Cecilia," he said impatiently. "Are you up for persuading her to give me the land? She's got a kid, and that might make it easier for you to convince her. I can't access the property unless she does it. There are new home communities going up all around this land, and if I'm spotted where I shouldn't be, there could be a serious problem."

What he was suggesting made me want to punch him in the face, but I was still outnumbered here.

"Right, yeah," I agreed, ready to get the hell out of there. "I'll take care of it."

"Good. I had a feeling I could count on you. Check in with me here next week. Let me know how it goes. In the meantime, just keep what I told you between us, or you'll go the same way Raymond did."

He said it lightly, as if he was just making conversation, not threatening my life.

"Of course," I said through gritted teeth.

"Now, let's get back to the warehouse. Your fight will be starting soon."

I didn't say anything as we turned around to make our way back to the warehouse. For once, I wasn't in the mood to fight at all.

MY DATE with Kat was that night. I didn't actually have a plan when I asked her out, but I knew that it should be something fun.

Luca slowed to a stop, and I was sure that he was on to me. My pulse raced, and I tried to figure out how to get away from these three men in one piece, but Luca surprised me.

"You know what? I like you, Blade. You're bold, an innovator. So, I'm going to let you in on a secret. It's all about location, location, location."

That wasn't exactly a secret when talking about real estate, but I wasn't going to correct him. Luca started walking again, quicker this time, but I kept pace with him.

"You see, there's something special about this location. Something that Cecilia doesn't know about. Her late husband was good at keeping secrets."

"Secrets?"

Luca leaned closer so that only I could hear. "Raymond Groves used that land to store weapons."

"What?" I couldn't have heard him right.

"Yep. Military-grade weapons, supposed to be worth hundreds of thousands of dollars."

"How do you know this?"

"I'll get to that. He got the stuff from a big-time arms dealer based in El Paso. The dealer smuggled the shit in from Mexico but needed a place to hide it while it was too hot to move. So he contacts a friend of a friend…"

"You mean Raymond Groves?"

Luca nodded, his eyes lit up with excitement. "So, Raymond takes it and tells the guy that he can hide on this unused piece of land he has."

"I still don't understand how you know all this."

"You know that arms dealer? His operation was taken over by my boss two months ago. You'd think a hardened criminal like him wouldn't talk, but I guess anyone with squeal if you push the right buttons."

"Have you ever hurt a woman?" Luca asked, not looking directly at me. His eyes roamed over our surroundings, always alert.

My stomach somersaulted. *What the fuck?*

The answer was no, but I was sure that wouldn't be what he wanted to hear. Whatever he wanted me to do had to be tied to this question.

"I believe in discipline," I replied. The words disgusted me, but I had a part to play here.

Luca laughed as if what I said was hilarious. He clapped me on the back like we were old pals.

"Me too," he said. "But some people don't think like you and me, which is how we end up with a problem."

"What kind of problem?"

"A mouthy little bitch by the name of Cecilia Groves."

Shit. That was Raymond Groves's wife, the woman that Outlaw Souls was supposed to protect.

"Tell me about her," I said, glad that my voice didn't betray anything going on in my whirring mind.

"She has something that I want, and *someone* has to persuade her to give it up."

"What is it?"

He smiled. "A primo piece of land just five miles north of La Playa."

My excitement nearly gave me away, making me keen to push for more information, but I forced myself to pause and take a deep breath. If I appeared too interested, he'd likely suspect something, and I'd end up with a bullet in my back before I even knew what happened. Luca's bodyguards were still tight on us.

"Why not just look into something else? If it's land you want, there's plenty in La Playa that could be obtained more easily."

I'd put my name in for that, knowing that they'd all seen me fight and knew what I was capable of. What they didn't know was that I wasn't into roughing up people that were indebted to Luca. I preferred a fair fight.

"Blade, it's good to see you here again," Luca said when Kane brought me to him. He was always removed from the crowd, on a wooden platform that I suspected was built for him to see the fights from his chair. He was like a king on his throne here, surrounded by men that openly carried their guns on their hips. I was packing tonight, too, but mine was tucked away, out of sight.

"Luca," I nodded in his direction, not getting close enough to shake his hand while that damn reptile was on him. "I hear you might have some work that I'd be suited for?"

Luca nodded. "I might. Depends on what you're willing to do."

"Whatever the boss tells me to do." I could tell that was the right answer by the look on Luca's face. This guy got off on being the big man in charge.

"Good. Walk with me."

Luca put his snake into an open tank on the floor beside him, and I remembered what Kane had said about him being eccentric. That was an understatement. He stood, and two of his men came forward, stopping just behind him as we walked together out of the warehouse. The street was dark, with cars parked in the unused lots of the warehouses around us to avoid drawing attention to our location. It seemed like a wasted effort when I realized that I could hear the crowd yelling at the fighters out here.

I followed his lead as we made our way west, moving closer to the docks, which were abandoned at this time of night.

TEN

BLADE

I went back to the fighting ring two more times this week. It was making me a crowd favorite since I won all my fights, but even more importantly, it gave me the opportunity to get close to Kane, which meant that I was getting closer to Luca.

I'd even seen the snake that Kane had told me about, a big yellow thing that I wasn't too proud to admit made me nervous. Luca came into the warehouse tonight with it draped around his neck like some living accessory. It made him look like the villain in a vampire movie or something ridiculous like that.

I came alone tonight for the first time. It made me feel jumpy, but the closer I got to Luca, the more uncomfortable I was with bringing Alex along. It was one thing for me to knowingly get close to a man that Outlaw Souls suspected to be a killer, but Alex didn't know what he was getting into. I couldn't tell him, so I didn't bring him.

I'd decided to work a new angle to get information. Kane had mentioned that Luca was looking for some muscle, a man that could do his dirty work for a big payday.

Jason hopped up from the couch and hugged me. "Thanks. You don't know what this means to me."

I hugged him back but pulled away after a few seconds and gave him a grave look. "You've got to figure out what matters more to you. Lexie or Las Balas. I know that you want to follow in Dad's footsteps and get closer to him by joining the club, but don't forget that the reason neither of us is close to him is that he put that club above his family, and it ruined his marriage."

"You don't understand. The club is like a family. They just want loyalty."

"Well, you can't keep putting Lexie on the back burner and expecting her to stick around. That's all I'm saying."

I could tell that he wanted to argue with me, but he wasn't really in a position to do so since I was doing him this favor. Instead, he thanked me again and left, eager to head home and tell Lexie that their plans for this weekend were still on.

Part of me felt that I shouldn't get involved in Jason's relationship like this. He had to figure this shit out for himself. But I didn't want my brother to be lonely like me. Without Lexie, he'd have no one, just the club.

Home alone once again, I considered going out, but Piper was on a date, and I didn't want to go alone. Blade's face flashed through my mind, but I quickly discarded that idea, as well. Our date was in two days, and I didn't want to go out with him before that. A night of drinking that would probably end in sex would be fun, but I felt like there was a potential for more with him. I'd rather wait and see what he had planned for Friday night.

"PLEASE, KAT," Jason's voice was whiny, and I rolled my eyes.

"No way."

"Come on, the future of my relationship depends on you."

"Why is that *my* responsibility?" I asked, exasperated. We were at my house again, but Jason wasn't visiting because of a fight with Lexie this time. It turned out that he'd promised to take her out this Saturday to make up for canceling their plans on her birthday, but, as usual, Las Balas was demanding his time instead. They wanted him to bartend at their bar, The Pit. They were supposed to have a band playing that night and expected a big turnout, so all prospects were expected to be there slinging drinks all night long.

"They told me that I could only get out of it if someone else covered for me. And they love you down there."

Yeah, some of the bikers loved me a little too much. They might have watched me grow up, but that didn't stop some of the older men from looking at me like a fresh piece of meat. Adding alcohol to the mix might even make a couple of them handsy. My dad would be there, but he wasn't the type to be protective.

"You'll probably make a killing in tips," Jason added, clearly pulling out all the stops to entice me to do this for him.

I considered it. It didn't sound like the ideal way to spend my Saturday, but at least I wouldn't be stuck at home alone. I could put the money I made toward my savings for a motorcycle. As for the men that hit on me, I felt pretty confident that I could take care of myself.

"Fine," I sighed. "I'll do it, just this once."

All I could imagine was getting horizontal with him, which sounded like plenty of fun.

"What do you have in mind?"

He shook his head, and his cocky smirk made its first appearance of the day. I was surprised by how much I missed it. "You'll just have to wait and see."

Okay, I was intrigued.

"When?"

"Friday night," he said, pulling his helmet onto his head. "After work. We'll take the bike, so dress accordingly."

I understood that to mean wearing pants. I'd learned that lesson the hard way as a teenager on the back of my dad's bike. I'd gone on a ride with him on a hot summer day, insisting on wearing shorts. After an hour on the road, we'd stopped for gas, and I had brushed against the screaming hot header pipe. The burn on my skin was instant and agonizing. I still had a scar on my calf from it.

I'd make sure to bring my helmet, too. I never got on a bike without one. I didn't give a damn if it was lame, as I had been told by some of the Las Balas members in the past. My dad had told me a story about a biker he knew that got into an accident without one on, and it was gruesome. I liked the shape of my skull as it was, thank you very much.

"Okay, but you better feed me. I'm not one of those girls that won't eat in front of a man."

Blade got onto his bike. "Don't worry, you'll be fed. You'll need the energy."

Heat locked in my lower belly at his words, but before I could form a response, he fired up the bike and rode away.

"Kat? Blade? You guys almost finished up back there?"

I ripped my mouth away from Blade's, mentally chastising myself for doing this here.

"Uh, ye-yeah." I cringed at the breathless quality of my voice. Blade stepped back, putting distance between us, and I made sure that my shirt was straight. My hair was pulled back in a ponytail today, so at least I didn't have to worry about mussed hair giving away what we were up to.

"You okay?" Her voice was closer.

I stepped to the side, putting more distance between myself and Blade. I ripped open the curtain to find that Brie was only a few feet away. I knew that it shouldn't thrill me to come so close to getting caught, but it did.

My lips were tingling from the feeling of Blade's kiss as I smiled at Brie.

"Just fine," I said chirpily.

Brie furrowed her brow as she looked between us, trying to figure out the weird vibe in the room. Finally, after several long seconds, her expression cleared.

"Good." She gestured to the front door. "Now, let's get the hell out of here."

We shuffled past her, going out the front door while she shut off the lights and locked up. Normally, Blade took off on his bike right away, but today, he lingered in the parking lot with me. We bid goodbye to Brie and watched as she got into her car and drove away.

"You know what I think, Kitten?" He didn't wait for me to guess before continuing. "I think it's time I took you on a date."

"Like dinner and a movie?"

"Come on, I think I can do better than that. We'll have some fun."

I started to leave, making it to the curtain that separated the front and back of the shop before I felt a strong grip on my arm, making me stop.

"I think you do care," Blade said, his voice a low rumble in my ear.

My heart pounded against my ribcage. His touch was sending a tingling sensation all over my body, and I found myself leaning back into him until our bodies were flush. I could feel an erection poking at my ass and wanted to grind into it, but I held back. If I started down that road, I wasn't sure I could stop. I was already so hot for him, and we'd barely touched yet. I could hear Brie on the other side of the curtain, cashing out the register while she hummed to herself. Knowing that she was so close made our contact feel risky and cranked up my desire further.

"Tell me, Kitten, have you been trying to figure me out all day?"

Damn him for being able to read me so easily.

I turned around so that we were face-to-face, our bodies still flush. He was hard in all the right places, and I wondered if he liked it rough.

"Maybe," I admitted. "But you don't seem to mind."

My eyes darted to his lips, and the next thing I knew, he took my mouth in a hard kiss. Blade's hand came up to the back of my neck, holding me in place.

But I wasn't going anywhere.

My lips molded to his, fire spreading through my veins. I raked my nails up his arm, wanting to moan at the taste of him when he licked his way into my mouth.

I couldn't remember the last time I'd been so turned on by a man, and the idea of taking this somewhere private was appealing. Before I could even consider doing it, Brie's voice brought me back to reality.

NINE
KAT

There was something different about Blade at work today. He was more reserved than I'd ever seen him. There were no teasing flirtations. I didn't know him well, and it might not even mean anything, but I couldn't shake the feeling that something was bothering him.

I took several customers in the morning and spent most of the afternoon finishing the full sleeve I'd started yesterday, so I had plenty to do to keep myself busy. But I had this awareness of Blade the whole time. It was like there was a connection between us that was impossible to ignore.

"What's up with you today?" I asked when the shop closed and we were getting ready to leave. Piper had a date, so she'd hurried through the cleanup and took off right away.

"What do you mean?" His tone was just a little *too* nonchalant to be believable.

"You're..." I searched to find a word, "broody."

"Am not."

"Whatever," I said, turning away from him. For some reason, his denial frustrated me. "I don't care, anyway."

hard to be close to her. Alex was the closest family I had these days, but he didn't even live in La Playa.

I knew that things would be different if Mark was still alive. My big brother had been the perfect child that my dad wanted. He was smart as a whip and willing to fall in line. When he died, he'd already signed up for the Army.

I wasn't Mark, and I never would be. Sometimes, I thought that my father's real problem was that he just couldn't forgive me for that.

good about my gift as she handled it carefully, looking over the ornate design, but it was ruined by my father.

"Looks a little expensive for you," he commented drily.

Asshole.

The shop keepers had treated me like that when I bought the thing, too. Looking at me with raised eyebrows and uninterested glances. Granted, I was dressed in my usual black jeans and white t-shirt, with my tattoos on full display and a helmet in one hand. So, I didn't look like I belonged in a shop full of delicate and expensive collectibles.

It still pissed me off, though.

"You don't know shit about my finances," I spat. His eyes darkened, and out of the corner of my eye, I registered the disappointment on my mother's face. I hated myself for being a part of the problem, but I couldn't bite back my anger now.

"I know *you*," he countered. "Your lack of discipline and irresponsibility are common knowledge, so you'll forgive me if I question your ability to buy something like this."

"No, actually, I won't."

I stood, taking a moment to remove my damn tie while both of my parents watched. I tossed it down on the table, glad to be rid of it.

"Sorry, mom. I gotta go." I didn't bother making up an excuse. We all knew what was going on here. "I'm glad you like the gift. And dad, if I'm such a fuck-up, I guess you better cover the cost of my dinner."

I left the restaurant with anger battling guilt for dominance. This kind of thing was the reason that I was eager to join the Outlaw Souls. I'd seen firsthand the way that they treat each other like family, and I wanted that. My mom was great, but the friction between my dad and me made it

I gritted my teeth. Why did he always have to push it with me?

"Let's just say that the boss and I had some fundamental differences."

"Translation, you pissed him off and got sacked."

"Harold," my mom placed a hand on his arm with a frown on her face. This always happened, no matter the occasion. We ended up bickering, and she was stuck in the middle.

"Fine," he grumbled, placing his larger hand on top of hers. "Tell us about the new job."

"I'm a tattoo artist at a little shop in La Playa."

He scoffed.

"You've always been so artistic. That's a great fit for you," my mom said, but I could see the concern in her eyes. "Do you make enough money there? Can we help you in any way?"

The look on my dad's face told me that he'd rather chew his own arm off than give me money.

"No, Mom. I do just fine."

It wasn't a lie. The cut that Brie took was small enough to allow me to make a decent living.

"Here," I handed over the gift. "I got you something."

"You didn't have to do that."

She tore open the wrapping paper, pulling out a white box. Inside, nestled among tissue paper, was an elephant figurine. She'd collected them for as long as I could remember, always looking for unique designs. This one was opulent with a headdress covered in Swarovski crystals and gems.

"Oh, Blade. It's beautiful."

There was a moment in which I allowed myself to feel

stand. He was always easy to spot, being so tall. And a man like Harold Shelton wasn't going to slouch self-consciously either. Nope, he walked with his head high and shoulders back, like the war hero that he was.

My mom was at his side, her blonde hair pulled back in a French twist. She smiled when she saw me waiting at the table. I stood to greet her, pulling her thin body into a hug while she kissed my cheek. She'd always been a small woman, seemingly fragile. I suspected that my father saw her the same way, and she had him wrapped around her little finger.

"Happy birthday, Mom," I said.

"I'm so glad you could make it," she said, stepping back, but keeping a hold of my hands. She looked me over with a small grin. "And you look so handsome."

"Here you go, Molly," my dad said, pulling out a chair for her.

Silence settled over the three of us as we all picked up our menus. I tugged at the knot of the tie around my neck, trying to loosen it a bit. My father's sharp eyes caught the movement, and I could see the judgment there, but I didn't care. I felt like I was suffocating with it on. How did some men wear them every day?

The waitress came to take our orders before scurrying away. The place was busy tonight and looked to be understaffed. My mom turned to me.

"Tell me how you're doing. It's been too long since we saw you."

"I've started a new job."

"What happened to the old one?" my dad interrupted.

"It didn't work out," I tried to be vague.

"Because?"

"Come on," I said to Alex, gesturing with my head to a spot further from the crowd. I needed to wrap my hands and shed my shirt.

"What the hell was that?" Alex asked in a demanding tone while following along behind me.

"Friendly small talk," I said without turning to look at him.

"Bullshit."

I sighed as I came to a stop. Turning to face Alex, I leaned in closer so that we wouldn't be overheard.

"All you need to know is that Luca is bad news. I'm trying to figure out what he's up to."

"Does this have anything to do with that club you're a part of?"

Sometimes I forgot how perceptive he could be.

"I'm not a member yet."

Alex let the subject drop, but I was sure that I would have to answer his questions eventually. For now, it was time to fight.

I TRIED NOT to fidget as I sat in the stiff wooden chair, waiting for my parents to arrive. Ocean's Edge was an upscale seafood joint, the kind of restaurant that required a jacket. It wasn't my kind of place, but I wasn't going to skip out on my mom's birthday dinner.

Sitting on the table at my elbow was a pretty little box covered in blue wrapping paper and a white bow made of ribbon. My parents didn't hurt for money, so I never knew what to buy her as a gift. She'd just tell me not to bother if I asked.

My eyes landed on my father's rigid form at the hostess

tion and would gossip about his employer as long as I didn't make him suspicious.

"Oh, you know. Weird interests, almost obsessions. Like his damn pet snake."

"Snake?"

"Yeah. You know, the one he wears around his neck sometimes. Big mother fucker."

Okay. We were getting off track now.

"The snake. Right." I had no idea what he was talking about, but it seemed like a good idea to play along. Kane took another drag off his cigarette.

"And lately, he's been obsessed with that piece of land."

Jackpot.

"Yeah? What land?"

Kane shrugged. "Some empty lot just outside of town. Nothing but a big empty field. Not sure what the hell his deal is with it, but all he's talked about lately is buying the damn thing. He had a fit the other night when that real estate guy told him he wouldn't sell it."

My stomach clenched. I couldn't believe that Kane was talking about the man that was murdered. It felt almost too good to be true, but I wasn't going to question it. My gut told me that this man was a good source of information, and it was right.

"Did Luca say anything else about that guy?" I asked as Kane tossed his cigarette butt onto the ground with the ember still lit. When he looked at me again, I could have sworn that I saw a hint of suspicion in his glassy eyes.

"You know, you ask a lot of questions." Kane looked between Alex and me. "You gotta thing for Luca, or what?"

I gave a weak smile as Kane laughed at his own inquiry. It looked like this conversation was over. Just in time, too. I was next to fight.

"Looking to score some blow," I said on a whim. In reality, I didn't touch that shit, but it would do well to hide my real motives. I saw Alex freeze out of the corner of my eye and hoped that he wouldn't interrupt unless I needed backup for some reason.

"Really?" Kane leveled me with a speculative gaze, which I met head-on. I wasn't sure what he was looking for, but I made sure that my eyes didn't waver.

"Yep. My friend and I are hoping to have a good time later tonight."

"Why'd you come to me?"

"You're Luca's man, right? I heard he supplies." That was a risk, but I needed to move this conversation forward.

"Where did you hear that?"

I gestured vaguely to the crowd around us. "Word on the street. But, you know what? Forget about it. I can take my business elsewhere."

I started to turn away, but Kane spoke.

"Stop." I did as he commanded, biting back a smile as he fell for my bluff. "I don't deal for Luca, but you can ask him directly."

I wasn't sure that was wise, but I didn't see that I had a choice.

"Where is he?"

Kane shook his head. "He's not here tonight. He has some business to take care of elsewhere."

"Is that so?"

Kane pulled a pack of cigarettes out of his pocket, lighting up one with a match. I watched as he inhaled before blowing out a puff of smoke.

"Luca's a busy man. Little eccentric, too, if you ask me."

"How's that?" I couldn't believe how lucky I was getting with this guy. I suspected that he liked having my full atten-

Alex took it without comment, and I tipped back my own drink. Usually, when I came here, I registered to fight, then stayed out of the way. I spent the time observing the fights, taking mental notes on my potential future opponents, and getting hyped up for my own round. I wasn't interested in making friends.

But tonight, I had to work the crowd.

I could feel the weight of Alex's gaze as I led us around the edge of the group of observers. Closer to the fighting ring, the crowd was rowdy, as the gamblers got worked up over the fight, but further back, I could have a conversation.

I spotted a man that I'd seen at Luca's side in the past. If I remembered correctly, he went by the name Kane. Approaching, I took note of his bloodshot eyes as he polished off a bottle of Bud, tossing the empty to the side, where it broke on the concrete along with a small pile of others. If they were all his, luck was on my side. In my experience, drunk men had loose lips.

"Who do you favor in the next fight?" I asked, stopping beside him and leaning against a concrete pillar.

If he was surprised that I was talking to him, he didn't show it.

"You planning to place another bet? It sure as hell worked out well for you last time." Kane remarked.

I shrugged. "Not sure. It's easy to bet on myself, but I can't predict what others will do."

"I'll admit, you surprised the hell out of me last week. The Beast is...well, a *beast*. I'm not sure if you're a hero around here or a villain for taking him down."

"I'm not here to make friends either way."

"So, why are you talking to me?"

Damn, he had me there. Maybe he wasn't as drunk as I'd hoped.

EIGHT
BLADE

The warehouse was full of people once again. The turnout for these street fights was huge, much larger than I would have guessed before I started coming. I figured that a secret, illegal activity like this would have to have a limited number of participants to keep it under wraps. It turned out that we were all at risk of incarceration just by being here, so no one was likely to rat out the location for fear of getting busted themselves. It was kind of beautiful.

"I can't believe you talked me into coming back here," Alex said from my side. He was in a shitty mood tonight.

The frustrating thing was that Alex probably would have been more willing to tag along and watch my back if he knew that I was trying to gather information about a killer to avenge a man and protect that man's wife and kid. But that was club business, and I couldn't talk about it.

"Lighten up. The guy I'm going up against tonight isn't nearly as big as the Beast."

"I still don't like it."

"Drink your beer and stick with me," I said, handing over a bottle with the cap already twisted off.

These days, with divorce rates being as high as they were, it seemed like setting yourself up for failure to me.

I never wanted to do it.

As Tammy talked about her plans for the wedding, which wasn't even going to take place until next year, I tried to look interested. I just couldn't wrap my head around spending so much money on one party that didn't really mean anything in the end. It was just a piece of paper that represented a promise that could easily be broken. Marriage didn't mean forever. The only way that was going to happen was if you wanted it.

Personally, I'd rather spend that kind of big money on a new bike or a vacation, something like that.

I thought about my empty house. It would be nice to have someone there, someone to come home to every day, but I didn't need a wedding band to know that I had that. I believed in a man showing his intentions with actions, not words and promises.

It couldn't have come at a better time. I needed the girl time.

"But will I learn to hide it before I go broke?" Piper asked.

I snickered.

There was a bowl of chips sitting between Tammy and me, and I kept snacking on it. I shouldn't have skipped dinner, but at least Veronica always provided snacks. Every time we met at my place, I was lucky to have a six-pack on hand. I'd endured endless teasing over the years for not being a good host.

"So, what's new in your world?" Tammy asked, shuffling to deal another hand.

"Same shit," I shrugged, but Piper nudged my side with a teasing grin.

"Don't lie," she said. Then, she addressed Tammy. "We have a new co-worker, and he's hitting it off with Kat already."

"Is love in the air?" Veronica asked, throwing five dollars worth of chips into the middle of the table.

"Hardly," I rolled my eyes. "He's hot, but I don't really know him yet."

"Speaking of love," Veronica looked at Tamy, "do you want to share your news?"

With the biggest smile I'd ever seem, Tammy held up her left hand, where a square-cut diamond sparkled on her finger.

"Bill finally popped the question?" Piper asked, leaning forward to get a better look at the rock.

"Yep." Tammy was glowing as she confirmed it.

"Congrats," I said. I was happy for her, but I didn't understand what the big deal was about getting married.

my body halfway inside of my vehicle, I saw Blade mounting his bike.

I'd love to ride on the back of it, my body pressing against his in all the right places, my thighs spread wide. The thought sent a wave of desire through my core. I figured that Piper was right about the sexual tension. I could only take so much before I snapped.

I LOOKED up from the cards in my hand to see Veronica walk into the room with a tray in her hands loaded up with a pitcher of frozen margaritas and salt-rimmed glasses. I was more of a beer drinker myself, but I'd never say no to a free drink.

"I made margaritas!"

Not that it was really *free*. I'd already lost about fifty bucks at this table in the last two hours. I was a shitty poker player, even though I played with these women often.

Piper was even worse than me. Sitting to my right, she had a small little half-smile that I knew meant she had a good hand. One-by-one, the other two women at the table folded. I did the same, and Piper pouted.

"I've told you, you have a tell," I said apologetically.

"Don't worry, Piper, you'll learn to hide it," Veronica said as she handed over a glass full of the alcoholic drink. We were at Veronica's house, enjoying a ladies' night poker game. Veronica was an old friend of mine from high school. We'd kept in touch over the years and started getting together occasionally for drinks after her divorce. That had evolved into a weekly poker night with Piper and Veronica's sister, Tammy.

of his finger to tilt my chin up until I was looking into his eyes.

"You'd like that, wouldn't you?" he asked.

I felt a shiver run down my spine. Yes, I wanted to know what made him tick, but I wasn't going to tell him that. That wouldn't be nearly as fun.

So, I straightened and took a step back. "Good night, Blade."

I winked at him before turning and walking over to Piper, who was waiting for me by the curtain with an amused expression on her face. She waited until we were outside to call me out on it.

"So, you want Blade, huh?"

"Maybe." There was no point in denying it. She worked right there with us.

Now that I thought about it, she'd been quieter than usual today. I looked at her out of the corner of my eye.

"You're not upset, are you?" I asked. "I mean, I don't want you to be uncomfortable."

"Girl, I'm just enjoying the show," she laughed. "The little game you two are playing is amusing as hell."

"Game?" I asked as we walked across the parking lot together, where our cars were parked side-by-side.

"The will-they-won't-they thing. The sexual tension between the two of you is gonna snap like a rubber band."

I laughed, but she was probably right.

"If that happens at work, I'm outta there," she declared.

I put an arm around her shoulders and gave her a squeeze. I wanted to tell her that I would never do that at the shop, but I had a feeling that when it came to Blade, all bets were off.

I was getting into my car when I heard the distinct rumble of a motorcycle engine coming to life. Turning with

For an intricate piece like this, I didn't want any distractions, so I selected my punk rock playlist on my iPhone and plugged in my earbuds. One song after another played as I went over the marks I'd made with the tattoo gun, working steadily. The client was my favorite kind to have in my chair, just content to relax and let me work without chattering or needing a lot of breaks. When he took his shirt off, I spotted several other tattoos on his body, so I figured this was just another, bigger one for him.

Time flew as I worked, and by the time I finished the outline, it was closing time. I scheduled him to come back tomorrow to finish the piece, rubbing my stiff hand from holding the tattoo gun for so long. It looked great, and I was excited to complete it with shading tomorrow.

"Wow. You were in the zone today," Blade said as we did our end of the day clean-up. It was the first time he spoke without coming across as cocky or teasing.

I smiled. "I love working on a nice piece like that."

"You mean the guy?" he asked. The teasing tone was back in his voice, but I could see something darker flash in his eyes.

"I mean the tattoo, doofus."

"Ouch." He placed a hand on his chest and pouted.

"Are you ever serious?"

"I try to keep things light," he shrugged.

I was finished with my clean-up, so I grabbed my purse out of the cabinet and walked over to the divider separating our sections.

"You know," I leaned forward on my elbows as he finished his own cleaning, "I have a feeling that you've got an edgier side, just beneath the surface."

Blade closed the distance between us and used the tip

SEVEN
KAT

Jealousy was an unfamiliar and ugly emotion. I wanted nothing to do with it.

But when I walked into the shop this morning and saw Blade with a topless Ashlynn, I had felt it. I knew it was crazy since we'd just met, but all I could figure was that I wanted to sleep with him. It made sense. He was my type. Confident. Sexy. Biker. Tattooed.

He checked all the boxes, and he seemed interested in me, too.

I was sure it was going to happen sooner or later. Why not? We'd have a few rounds between the sheets, and I'd get him out of my system.

I thought about it all morning. Then, a man came in just after my lunch break, interested in a full sleeve. He wanted me to design one that would look like he had a robot arm under his flesh. We spent the better part of an hour just working on the design. I drew it out on a sketchpad that I kept on hand for just this kind of thing. Once he was happy with it, I drew the outline on his skin, until he had pen marks from shoulder to wrist.

"Thanks for the advice. But it's not necessary. I have a type. Barbie isn't it."

"Really? And why would I care?" she challenged, but I could see the spark of interest in her eyes.

"Just making friendly conversation," I said. I could tell that Piper was listening, so I didn't say any of the filthy things that were running through my mind as I peeked down the front of her top. "Personally, I like a woman with a wild side."

"You think you can handle that?"

I wasn't too sure anymore as I looked into her blue eyes. It looked like I might have met my match. But I was determined to find out, one way or the other.

top that showed off her breasts so thoroughly that I couldn't help but stare.

"You know, when a client takes off their clothing, we usually close the curtains around our workspace," Kat said, pointing to the track that ran in a circle above my head.

"She ripped the shirt off without warning," I shrugged. "I take it she's not exactly the shy type."

"Good news for you, I guess," she muttered as she tucked her purse away in a cabinet and set the coffees on the counter.

"What's that supposed to mean?" I asked.

"Nothing at all," her polite smile was back, and I didn't find it nearly as amusing when it was directed at me. "But here's some friendly advice—don't fuck the clients. It's bad for business."

I smirked. "What about the coworkers?"

Kat's eyes widened, but before she could form a response, the curtain was opened once again. Piper had arrived. She paused as she entered, staring between the two of us.

"Am I interrupting something?"

"Nope," Kat answered, a little too quickly.

I just smiled before pulling out an alcohol wipe from one of my drawers and deliberately wiping the phone number off my hand. I could see Kat watching me out of the corner of my eye.

"One of those coffees for me?" Piper asked, and Kat jolted.

"Oh...yeah. Here."

If I didn't know any better, I'd say that I was distracting her. She handed over one of the coffees to Piper, and I walked over to the little half-wall that separated us.

Ashlynn turned around to face me, also moving closer. Her breasts were only inches from my chest. I took a small step backward, trying not to be too obvious about putting distance between us. The last thing I wanted was for Kat to get the wrong idea. Not that I should care about that. Hadn't she just ridden off into the sunset with some guy right in front of me yesterday?

"Is this your first tattoo?" I asked Ashlynn.

"Yeah. Isn't it great? It's about how I try to live my life."

You and about a billion other people.

"New tattoos will look slightly faded while they're healing. It's because the top layer of skin peels off. It'll look better when it's completely healed."

"You're sure?"

I nodded. "Absolutely. If it still looks faded in a couple of weeks, come back, and we can fix it."

"*I* can fix it," Kat corrected. "It's my work."

"Of course." I couldn't help smiling. I liked it when she was worked up. Something about it made my skin feel tight.

"Okay, then," Ashlynn said, somewhat reluctantly. She grabbed her shirt off the black chair and tugged it on. "I didn't catch your name."

"I'm Blade," I said, holding my hand out for her to shake. Instead, she grabbed me by the wrist and picked up a pen from the counter beside me. I watched as she wrote down her phone number on the palm of my hand.

"Call me," she said, giving me a wink before turning around and sauntering out through the curtain.

Wow.

She was bold, I'd give her that. Too bad that she wasn't my type.

Kat made a disgusted noise in the back of her throat that drew my attention to her. Today, her shirt was a corset-style

"Ashlynn," she beamed as she walked into my work area. "Call me Ashlynn."

"Okay, Ashlynn, take a seat."

Brie mouthed a *thank you* to me before walking back to the front of the shop. It looked like I'd just earned a few brownie points from the boss.

Ashlynn didn't say another word before she reached down to the hem of her shirt and whipped it off over her head. My eyes darted to her chest—I was only human, after all—and I saw a hot pink bra, but I quickly returned my attention to her face.

"It's on my shoulder," she explained, turning to show me the words *Live, Laugh, Love* on her shoulder blade in big, curvy letters with a pink ribbon woven through them. It wasn't exactly the most complex tattoo I'd ever seen, but Kat did a good job with it. It was nice, clean work.

"Do you see how faded it is?" Ashlynn asked, looking at me over her shoulder. She had abandoned the whining and was acting like a damsel in distress now. I had a feeling that she thought it was seductive. Maybe that worked on other guys, but not me.

"I see a little color fading, but this looks fresh," I said as my eyes traced the edge of the tattoo, where the ink met her untouched skin. It was reddened and a little swollen. "Make that *very* fresh."

"She did it yesterday."

"Yes, I did. What's the problem?" Kat asked as she walked through the curtain with two styrofoam coffee cups in her hands.

There was a polite mask on her face when she looked at Ashlynn, and I bit back a chuckle. Kat did *not* like this girl.

"It's nothing," I answered before Ashlynn could. "Just a little normal color fade."

I glanced at the clock on the wall. "Don't we open in ten minutes?"

"Yeah, but the girls like to show up at the last minute." She seemed unconcerned about that.

I headed back through the curtain and into my workspace. I had left my portfolio behind yesterday so that I had it on hand for clients that wanted to see my work, but I already had two people coming in today for large pieces. It was amazing how easy it was to advertise for this kind of thing online. When I worked at the tattoo shop eight years ago, social media wasn't nearly as popular as it was today.

I had just sat down when I heard a commotion at the front of the shop. Before I could go investigate, the red curtain was ripped open, and a Barbie wannabe came marching through, followed by a harassed-looking Brie.

"You can't just come back here like that," Brie told the skinny blonde.

"She's really not here?" The girl sounded confused as she looked in the direction of Kat's workspace.

"I told you that," Brie said, crossing her arms across her chest.

"But she has to do something," Blondie said, her voice took on an unappealing whining quality. "The tattoo doesn't look right anymore. She must have messed it up."

"Maybe I can help you," I offered. I barely knew Kat, but I bet that she wouldn't take kindly to the suggestion that she had messed up. If I could diffuse whatever this situation was before she arrived, that might be for the best.

"Do you do tattoos?" she asked as her eyes flickered over me. I could see the interest in her expression as her gaze took in my muscular arms.

"Yep. So, why don't you take a seat and show me the problem, Miss..."

"What do you want from me?" I asked.

"We can't go after him for retribution until we know his plan. Taking him out before then is reckless."

"So...undercover work?"

Ryder smiled. "Exactly."

Now, as I sat in my sunny kitchen eating a second bowl of cereal, the heaviness of that conversation felt unreal, but I knew what was expected of me.

No one wanted to put me in danger, so I was to keep doing the same thing I had been, to avoid suspicion. I had to keep going to the fights a couple of times a week. But now, I had to snoop around to see what I could find out about Luca. There were always dozens of people in the crowd, and surely one of them knew the man well enough to provide answers. I just had to find him and get him to talk.

I fired off a text to Alex, asking him to come with me again on Saturday. Trainer wanted to come to watch my back, but I was worried about bringing yet another new face to the warehouse. It might look suspicious. Of course, Alex might say no. He'd been in a pissy mood the last time, so it wouldn't surprise me. He didn't reply right away, so I slipped on my boots and headed out the door.

It wouldn't do to be late on my first full day of work.

I owned a motorcycle and a car, but I rode the bike as much as possible. Nothing could compare to the feeling of being on a bike. It was exhilarating, a thrill that I didn't get from any other mode of transportation.

When I got to Ink Envy, there was only one other car in the lot, and I recognized it as Brie's. Sure enough, when I walked inside, she was in her spot at the counter, flipping through a magazine.

"You're here early," she said, looking pleased.

elbows on the table, "and we have concerns about his activities."

"You know that we've taken strides to be a more legitimate organization in the last few years," Trainer added. "We don't deal drugs or sell guns in La Playa, and we try to stop others from doing it."

"We've had a lot of success with it," Ryder continued. "But that means that someone could see an opening, an untapped potential to peddle their product."

"And that's what you think Luca is doing?" I asked.

"I'm sure of it," Ryder answered confidently. "But my greater concern is that he might be involved in the murder of Raymond Groves."

The surprises kept on coming. Raymond was a developer that owned a lot of land on the outer edge of La Playa, where he was building new homes in subdivisions to sell. The man had money, and it was assumed that money had something to do with his death.

But I didn't understand what Luca or the Outlaw Souls had to do with this.

"Raymond wasn't just a developer, he was a realtor. He worked with us to obtain the apartment complex and was a friend of the club."

I knew what that meant. He was under the club's protection.

"So," Ryder said, "his death is an insult to us, and we are responsible for keeping his wife safe. We have reason to believe that Luca is the killer, and we need to know what he's up to."

I didn't ask why they believed this. The club had resources, including tech whizzes like Hawk. I trusted the members of this club. If they said he did it, that was good enough for me.

thought of our duties as bitch-work, but I never said that out loud.

But last night, when the meeting had broken up, Trainer had pulled me aside, telling me to stick around. I did, and when everyone else had left, the president of the club, Ryder, had come to get us. I was led into the room at the back of the bar where they had their meetings.

I'd never been in there before. It was a simple space, almost bare except for a couple of long wooden tables and the trash can that was now overflowing with beer cans and bottles. Ryder closed the door behind us, and when I turned, I saw that there was one more thing in the room. Hanging on the wall by the door was the club's insignia. The words *Outlaw Souls* curved around the image of a motorcycle, forming a circular shape.

Trainer took a seat at a table, so I followed suit, wondering what the hell this was about as I planted my ass in the seat beside him. When Ryder sat down across from me, his expression was solemn.

"What can you tell me about Luca Bianchi?" he asked.

I couldn't have been more surprised if he'd slapped me. Luca? Why would they want to know about him?

"Uh...I don't know much."

"But you've been participating in that fighting ring he has in the warehouse by the docks?"

"Yeah." I'd made no secret of it. Hell, I came to the Blue Dog right after my last fight. "But I don't exactly hang with the guy. He pays me when I win. That's it."

Ryder and Trainer exchanged a long look.

"What's going on?" I asked, trying not to sound impatient.

"He's a new player in town," Ryder said, leaning his

La Playa. It was a gorgeous ride, even taking the back roads. The ocean was constantly on one side, and the other side was mostly valleys and farmland with the far-off Blackridge Mountains as a backdrop.

"Who will be there?"

"Just the three of us."

Fuck.

It was always better to have a few extra people around when my dad and I got together to act as buffers. The two of us had a history of arguing and ruining family events. I didn't want to do that to my mom.

"Be at Ocean's Edge at seven."

He hung up before I even responded. He was such a damn ball of sunshine.

I opened my dresser drawers, randomly pulling out clothing. Yanking on my jeans, I scoured my mind, trying to figure out what my mom might want as a gift. If I remembered correctly, she was turning fifty, which was a big deal.

I was close to my mom. While I didn't get along well with my dad, my mom provided me with the unconditional love that one would expect from a parent. Sometimes I felt like a screw-up, and my dad hardly ever discouraged that thinking, but my mom was never like that. I might not deserve it, but she was my biggest fan.

When I was dressed in jeans and a black t-shirt, I went into the kitchen to scrounge up some breakfast. My brown hair was so short that it was already dry, and there wasn't anything there to style. That was the main reason that I had trimmed it so short with an electric razor. I wasn't interested in messing with it every day.

I poured myself a bowl of sugary cereal and thought about last night while I ate it at the kitchen table. Normally, Axel and I weren't directly involved in club business. I

SIX
BLADE

I was just stepping out of the shower, with water running in rivulets down my body, when my cell phone started ringing in the next room. I snagged a towel off the rack and raced out into the bedroom, only to scowl at it when I saw the name on the caller ID. Still, I accepted the call, sure that he'd just call again if I ignored him. He always got his way.

"Hey, Dad," I said with a sigh. Putting the call on speakerphone, I set the phone down on my dresser and started drying off.

"William." He already sounded tense, and it was only seven in the morning.

"Blade, Dad. I go by Blade."

"That's not the name your mother and I gave you. Speaking of your mother, I'm sure you know her birthday is next week."

I *didn't* know that, but I probably should have.

"Okay. What's the plan?"

"I want you to meet us for dinner on Sunday. Bring a gift."

My parents lived in Santino Bay, just two hours north of

something intangible like that. But what good would that do?

I left the book on the unmade bed and crossed to the closet. Opening it, I saw an untidy pile of shoes on the floor and rows of dresses hanging above them. It was nothing special. I should just box it all up and donate it. I could turn this room into a guest bedroom. It was meant to be the master suite, so it was bigger than my room, but I didn't think I could ever claim it as my own.

And then what would I do? Redecorate the living room? The kitchen? Erase all traces of my mom and move on with my life? Maybe that was the healthy thing to do, but it made everything real. I knew that I was weak, but I didn't want to face that reality yet.

So, I walked out of the room, closing the door behind me. I grabbed a bottle of beer from the kitchen and continued outside, resuming my seat on the patio. I was tempted to go out, but I felt like I had to prove something to myself. I could spend the evening here alone.

It might be the best way to begin moving on.

Yet, deep loneliness echoed inside of me. I just wasn't sure what to do about it.

Jason left while I was clearing the table, suddenly eager to get home to Lexie. At least some good came from this.

Damn, I wanted a cigarette.

Instead, I popped a stick of gum into my mouth, glad that I had thrown out every pack I had in the house when I committed to quitting. I knew myself well enough to know that I would cheat if there was a single cigarette in the house.

Now that I was alone, the house was too quiet. So, I tried flipping through the TV channels, but Jason's words lingered in my mind. I knew that he was right, but I felt like I was still reeling from the news of her death, unable to fully believe that she was never going to walk through the door again. It had been six months; shouldn't this get easier?

"Fuck it," I said out loud to myself.

I walked down the hall in the back of the house, passing by my bedroom and opening the door at the end of the hall. The room looked the same as it did the day my mom left and never came back. It was just like any other day. I was at Ink Envy while she ran errands. She was at the pharmacy when she collapsed.

It was a brain aneurysm. The coroner said that she probably had it for years without even knowing. It ruptured, and she was gone before she even hit the floor. I supposed that should've been a comfort, but everything felt too surreal.

I crossed the room, taking a seat on the bed. There was a romance book upside down on the nightstand, only halfway finished. I picked it up, closing it. As I ran my fingers over the cover, I felt a wave of burning anger. I didn't have an outlet for it, knowing that there was no one to blame for what happened.

Unless I wanted to lay the blame on fate or God or

Yeah, she could. I looked across the round table at the chair beside Jason. It was where she always sat, because it was the closest to the back door, just in case she needed to go inside for anything. I never thought about her not being here until she was already gone. Now, I felt like nothing in my life would ever be the same.

"You know," Jason said after a long moment of silence between us, "I think it's about time that you started making this house your own."

"It *is* mine," I said. I'd lived here my whole life, and Jason already had a home with Lexie. He and I agreed that I should keep it.

"Sure, it's yours on paper," Jason agreed, "but you haven't changed a thing. It's like she's still here."

"I wish she was."

Jason reached across the table, putting his hand over mine. "I do, too. But you can't keep this place like a shrine to her. It's your home, and you don't even want to be here."

I scowled. "You're too smart for your own good, you know that?"

"It's a blessing and a curse."

I sighed. "I hear you, but it's not easy."

"Have you at least started on her room yet?"

"I don't want to talk about this anymore," I said, picking at my potato salad with my fork. "I'll get to it in my own time."

"I'm just saying-"

"I said no." My words came out harsh, but I didn't take them back.

The rest of our dinner was awkward, with the heavy weight of the topic I refused to discuss hanging over us. I hated the tension in the air, but I couldn't talk about this. Didn't he understand that I wasn't ready?

seating area, with a glass-topped table and cushioned chairs. Beyond the concrete patio, there was a privacy fence around the yard, which was perfect for sunny spring days when I wanted to lay out on a lawn chair in my bikini without the neighbor's teenage son gawking at me. Along the west side of the yard, my mom had always had a vegetable garden. She grew tomatoes, cucumbers, and fresh herbs back there, often sending me out to grab a handful of basil or dill while she was in the middle of preparing dinner.

I didn't have her green thumb, and it made me sad to know that there would be nothing growing in that patch of dirt this year. Out front, there were flower beds along each side of the porch steps. With the warm spring weather, there were already Hosta plants growing up out of the ground, since they came back every year. Each day, when I left the house, I saw them, and it made me happy. I wasn't fit to carry on the tradition of planting big beautiful flowers in the garden, but at least I still had her perineal Hostas.

Jason joined me out on the patio, his arms laden with hamburger buns, plates, ketchup, and a container of potato salad. It wasn't extravagant, but we weren't fancy people. Sitting at the patio table, we dug in. Jason took a big bite and let out a moan.

"Damn, Kat. How do your burgers always taste so good?"

"Top secret recipe," I teased, fighting back a smile.

He threw his napkin at me across the table. "Don't be a dick. Just tell me."

I rolled my eyes at his insult. "Fine. I add garlic powder and seasoned salt to the meat. It's the way mom made her burgers. And what she put on the steaks."

Jason let out a low whistle. "She could make a killer steak."

to do anything in the kitchen. He was a terrible cook, too easily distracted.

He settled in on the couch while I worked and turned on some kind of History channel show about presidential assassinations. I could see the TV from the kitchen island due to the open concept of the rooms, and it was interesting, but I soon found my mind wandering.

When I met Blade today, I found myself attracted to a man for the first time in months. It wasn't just physical, although he *did* have that going for him with his stubble beard and dark eyes. I usually went for guys with long hair, something I could grab onto during sex, but Blade's close-cropped cut worked for him.

It was his personality that got to me. The guy had a swagger, and during our short interaction, I had gotten a glimpse of his confidence. That had always been my sweet spot with men, enough self-assurance to be attractive without crossing the line into being a cocky asshole.

He'd only been at the shop for a few hours today, observing, and I had clients most of the time to keep me busy. There was a constant awareness prickling at me, though, letting me know that he was watching me. I kept telling myself that it was just a professional curiosity kind of thing, but that didn't stop my body from responding to him. My skin felt more sensitive, and the juncture between my legs ached.

It had been way too long since I'd had sex.

Pushing thoughts of Blade to the back of my mind, I took the plate full of hamburger patties out to the grill. The outdoor space was my favorite part of this place, and I suspected that it was the reason that my mom had bought this house in the first place.

There was a covered patio where we kept our grill and

FIVE
KAT

The ride home from work was uneventful. Jason had bought me a new tire to replace the one that was flat, and the spare was back in my trunk. He didn't even complain or try to get out of it, to my surprise. Jason didn't usually have much money, but he'd managed to fork over the cost of a new tire *and* installation on short notice. It was odd, but when I questioned it, he blew me off. His demeanor reminded me of when he was questioned about Las Balas. He always got so damn evasive.

Jason still hadn't been back home, and when he asked to stick around for dinner, I knew that he was avoiding it. But he couldn't run away from his problems forever. So, despite my hatred of an empty house, I told him that I would only cook dinner for us if he promised to leave afterward and make up with Lexie.

So, I stood in the kitchen, forming raw hamburger meat into round patties. I was no Martha Stewart, but I could grill up a couple of cheeseburgers for us just fine. Jason half-heartedly offered to help, but I knew better than to ask him contribute it to poor decision making on my part. I watched as he went inside with the others, leaving me leaning against the building while Axel paced around. The guy always seemed to have a ton of energy that he was trying to burn off. When we first met, I thought he might be a tweaker, but now I knew that he just didn't like sitting still. His overactive mind wouldn't allow him to chill out.

It could get annoying, but I never called him out on it. I was here to watch over the most valuable property of the club, and I was going to do it, no matter who I was with. Hopefully, I'd earn my place and get to attend the meetings soon. I wanted to have a sense of brotherhood with these men. I was ready to wear an Outlaw Souls patch.

minutes for the Outlaw Souls meeting. My sex life would have to wait. I arrived with no time to spare. Everyone's bikes were already in the parking lot when I parked. I caught the eye of my sponsor for the motorcycle club, Trainer.

He was a big guy with a full beard and long hair. He looked like trouble, with his closed-off expression and large stature, but the truth was, he was a great guy. Trainer was a devoted husband and father to two kids that turned him into a big softie when they were around.

I had bought my bike off him months ago, a Sportster with the prettiest red paint job I'd ever seen. The thing was a hell of a smooth ride, both in town and on the highway. He bought bikes cheap and fixed them to be resold, and he was good at his job. I loved my motorcycle and had gotten to know Trainer when I bought it.

He was the Road Captain of the club and nominated me to become a prospect. It wasn't fun, I had to admit. There were two of us, myself and Axel. We did all the grunt work for the club but hadn't earned any of the rewards yet. It reminded me of pledging to join a fraternity. You had to do whatever they said and prove yourself. Until then, you weren't directly involved in club business. Tonight, Axel and I would be keeping watch over the bikes during the Outlaw Souls meeting.

It was dull unless someone got stupid enough to try to mess with the motorcycles. Outlaw Souls were good people, overall, but that didn't mean you wanted to piss them off.

"Cutting it close, aren't you?" Trainer asked when I joined him in front of the building.

"Yeah, I got a job today at a tattoo shop. I just left."

"Good for you. Just try to stay out of trouble."

Trainer knew about my bad luck, although he tended to

"Is that why someone busted up your lip?"

I reached up and ran a thumb over the fresh wound. The swelling had gone down since last night, but the skin was still split and would take a couple of days to heal.

"What can I say? I'm a charmer."

Kat snickered, and the bell above the door announced the arrival of another customer. I looked around and realized that Brie had already left, presumably resuming her position at the front counter.

I spent most of the rest of the day watching Kat and Piper work, getting a feel for the way things were run around here. Perusing the drawers, I was impressed by how well-stocked they were. Brie ran a tight ship around here, and I had a feeling that I was going to fit in well. As long as I didn't screw it up somehow. My eyes lingered on Kat.

Yeah, it was probably not a good idea to go there.

This was confirmed when the end of the day arrived, and we were all leaving. Looking around the parking lot, I saw that there were only two cars and my bike. I opened my mouth to ask if someone needed a ride, but before I got the words out, a man on a Harley pulled into the parking lot.

He pulled up in front of the four of us, and Kat stepped forward.

"See you guys tomorrow," she said and pulled a helmet on. I watched her wrap her hands around the man's waist, and my gut clenched.

I told myself that there was no reason to care if that guy was her boyfriend. I just met this woman. Sure, she was sexy, but there were plenty of good-looking women out there. I didn't need to get hung up on Kat. I wasn't a one-woman kind of man, anyway.

I glanced at the time on my phone and hurried to my own motorcycle. I was expected to be at the Blue Dog in ten working on and was talking to the man in her chair. Her back was to me, so I still couldn't see her face.

"Don't bother with a bandage," the man said, but she shook her head.

"Not gonna happen, just like I told you last time. You leave here with the bandage. After that, it's up to you if you want to keep it on or not. But I suggest you don't be a dummy."

I smiled. I liked her attitude.

Kat didn't walk her customer out of the shop. Instead, she pushed her stool over to the counter to take a massive swig of a canned energy drink while he made his way to the door himself. That was when I got my first look at her.

Long dark eyelashes surrounded shockingly blue eyes. I trailed my eyes over high cheekbones and full lips. When she stood, I saw that her black tank-top and skintight jeans left little to the imagination, showing every slight curve on her thin body.

Damn.

I wasn't expecting to be hit with a fireball of lust in the first ten minutes of my new job, but there wasn't a thing I could do about it. This chick was hot.

And we were going to be working just feet away from each other.

"Take a picture.It'll last longer," she said with a little smirk.

I laughed lightly. "You've been holding onto that since the fifth grade or what?"

"Kat, this is the new tattoo artist," Piper interrupted, reminding me that she was still there. "Blade, this is Kat."

"Blade?" Kat repeated with a quirked brow. "That's...*unique.*"

"What can I say, I'm one of a kind."

walked out with a burly man following close behind her. There was a large bandage on his shoulder.

"Now, keep the bandage on for two hours and use the aftercare cream," the woman was saying as they walked past us. She had short, dirty blonde hair and a little too much makeup on for my taste.

I finished signing the papers as she walked the man to the door. Brie called her over to us.

"Piper, this is Blade, our new tattoo artist."

"Gary's replacement?"

"Yep."

"Nice to meet you," I said.

"It really is. I think we've already covered all the appointments he had scheduled, but it'd be nice to have some help with walk-ins."

"Let's take him back then," Brie said, coming around the counter.

I followed them through the curtain and saw the space was divided into three sections. There was another woman bent over a man's wrist with a tattoo gun in her hand in one of the sections. I couldn't see much of her, just a curtain of dark hair that was shielding her face.

"That's Kat," Piper said, nodding at the woman. She didn't look up at the sound of her name. I didn't blame her. I recognized an artist in the zone.

"Here's where you'll work," Brie gestured to the obviously unused workspace. It was pretty basic. A long counter with drawers that probably held the tattoo gun and other supplies, with an adjustable black leather chair in the middle and stool that must have been meant for me. It was a nice setup.

"Here you go, Jack," a voice said behind me. I turned to see that Kat was finished with the tattoo she had been and the low murmurs of conversation coming from the other side.

Finally, Brie closed the folder and looked up at me. "This is some good work."

I was relieved to hear that, but I braced myself for her to question the gaps in my employment, starting with the reason I left my old tattoo shop, but she didn't.

"Now, as a tattoo artist here, you'd really be a subcontractor, with me taking thirty percent off the top. The rest of your earnings belong to you. The clients would be yours, and you have freedom there. I know that this is art, and I'm not going to get in the way of it. Regardless of your appointments, I would like for you to be here during regular business hours for walk-ins, which are Monday through Friday, nine to six. Does that work for you?"

"Really? It's that easy?"

"Of course," Brie gave me a small smile. "I think you're talented. That's all I really need to know."

I grinned. This was the easiest job interview I'd ever had. "Hell yeah, that works for me."

"Good. Just one more thing. I don't want drugs of any kind here. No buying, selling, or using them in the shop. I don't want that shit here."

"No problem," I said without hesitation. I smoked a little pot on occasion, but I wouldn't even think to do that at work, and I'd never been interested in trying anything more intense. I'd seen too many people in my life get addicted to everything from crack to heroin.

It wasn't worth it.

Brie pulled out paperwork, and I signed on the dotted line. Just like that, I was employed. While we were taking care of the papers, the curtain pulled back, and a woman of the shop, the first thing I noticed was how clean and white everything was. There was a lot of love that went into this place.

There was a woman sitting on a stool behind a glass counter where there were rows of jewelry on display. I spotted earrings, nose studs, and tongue rings. I had numerous tattoos, but piercings weren't my thing. They looked hot on a woman, though.

I turned my attention to the woman behind the counter, who was watching me curiously. She was an older woman, probably in her forties, with two full sleeves covering her pale skin, and her long, brown hair was in dreadlocks.

"You must be William," she said, and I tried not to cringe at the use of my real name. My dad was the only one that called me that these days, but my friend Hawk had insisted that it was necessary to use my legal name on a resume, and I had sent mine when I replied to the job listing online.

"Yeah, but everyone calls me Blade," I said, reaching out to shake her hand as she stood.

"I'm Brie. I own Ink Envy."

"Nice place," I said, meaning it.

"Is that your portfolio?"

"Oh, yeah," I handed it over, mildly surprised that we were doing this here instead of in an office.

Brie opened the leather folder on top of the glass case, and I stood there awkwardly while she flipped through the pages. She stopped to stare at some pictures for several seconds and barely seemed to glance at others. She asked no questions, and I had no idea how this was going.

There was a big red curtain just beyond the counter that I guessed led to back rooms where the work was done. I could hear the unmistakable sound of tattoo guns buzzing was temporary. The army kept my dad moving around too much, which uprooted all our lives. My mom was more understanding than me, but she'd signed up for that life when she married him. I didn't have much of a choice.

So, suddenly, living on my own at the young age of eighteen had been exciting. I could finally settle somewhere. I threw myself into the job at the tattoo shop, starting by working closely with a seasoned tattoo artist, learning everything the older man knew. It came easily to me, and I was working on my own within three months.

I liked the work, but I always had a knack for finding trouble. After less than a year, I got locked up for six months for stealing a car. I hadn't even really wanted the thing, but I was trying to impress a girl. It worked, but by the time I got out of jail, she had moved on, and my spot at the shop had been replaced.

I was young and stupid back then. At least it was the only thing on my record.

Since then, I had worked various jobs, but I still owned a tattoo gun and did the occasional tattoo for a reasonable price out of my home. Going back to it as a job felt like a good move.

I pulled my bike into a spot in the parking lot, pulling off my helmet and checking out the artwork on the side of the building. *Fancy.*

Even from the outside, Ink Envy was completely different from that last shop I'd worked in. That place was small, old, and dark. I was pretty sure it wasn't even remotely up to code. Hell, it probably wasn't registered as a business.

By comparison, this place was *swanky*.

I grabbed the portfolio out of my saddlebag, filled with pictures of some of my best work. Walking through the door

FOUR

BLADE

I needed to find a job. The street fighting could be lucrative, but it was far from a steady paycheck. I had a sweet setup at my old job, working on the demolition crew of a construction company—which also helped me to work out my aggression—but I had been unceremoniously fired when I slept with my boss's wife.

In my defense, she hit on me.

Luckily, I had a broad skill set. As I pulled up to the little tattoo shop that was hiring, I couldn't help thinking about the little hole-in-the-wall place where I had first learned how to use a tattoo gun. That had been a small shop in a northern Californian city, where I'd lived right after graduating high school eight years ago.

After failing to enlist as was expected of me, I'd left my father's house. He was going to charge me rent to keep living there anyway—I was now an adult, after all, and he was a vindictive ass—so it wasn't worth putting up with his attitude just to stay in a house that I didn't even care about.

I'd learned not to get attached to people or places when I was young. Every new school, new friend, and new house been special and some of my best work, in my own opinion. "So, I was thinking I want the words live, laugh, and love on my shoulder blade."

I wanted to roll my eyes. Could she have picked a more generic phrase?

Whatever.

"Okay, let's pick colors."

Whether I liked the girl's choice or not, it was time to get to work.

"Make it seven," I said, thinking about all of the extra work I would have to do to make up for Gary's absence.

"Got it."

As he rode away, I walked into the shop to be greeted by Brie and a customer already waiting. I was right on time, so it was a surprise to see a customer had beat me to the shop. Looking into her face, I could see her eagerness.

"Kat, this is Ashlynn. She had an appointment with Gary for today, so you'll need to fill in," Brie explained.

"I wish Gary was still here. He was so hot," Ashlynn pouted, and I had to make sure that my thoughts didn't show on my face. Her voice was grating, reminding me of a valley girl. It was too early to deal with this shit.

"Well, it's just us girls now," I said, taking a sip from the bottle of water I had grabbed from my refrigerator before leaving the house. I wouldn't tell him because it would give him a big head, but Jason was right about dehydration. "Come on back."

I shot Brie an exasperated look, and she suppressed a smile. Apparently, she thought it was funny to start my day with this chipper princess.

"This is my very first tattoo, and I'm so excited that I'm getting it before my sister's wedding, so everyone will see it in my strapless dress," she prattled on and on as we walked through the curtain and into my workspace. "Does it hurt really bad? My bestie has one on her foot, and she said she cried when she got it."

My headache was starting to come back.

"Why don't you have a seat and tell me what you want?"

"Okay. I wanted something really special to me, you know?" I thought about the memorial I'd done last week for a man that lost his wife and wanted to honor her. That had cabinet and shake three pills out into my hand. I took them with some water from the tap and brushed my teeth.

Turning on the water in the shower stall, I ran it as hot as I could stand it, then stepped in, letting it wash over me, getting rid of the sand that managed to cover every inch of me. I couldn't linger too long, but by the time I shut off the water and stepped out, I felt rejuvenated, and there wasn't a single grain of sand left on my body.

My headache was still there, but it had diminished to a dull ache that I could live with. By the time I emerged from the bathroom, I was running short on time. So, I dressed in a flash, but when I went to grab my purse, my car keys were no longer sitting next to it.

"What the hell, Jason?" I asked. He was the only person here, so he must have taken them.

"I need the car if you want me to replace the tire," he explained. "Or are you going to let me off the hook for that one?"

"Not a chance."

"Then, let's go. We'll take my bike."

That sounded good to me. I grabbed my helmet, a full-faced white one, out of my coat closet and followed him outside. It was a great day for riding, with almost no wind blowing and the sun shining down on us.

I loved springtime.

I used to have my own bike, a small Suzuki 650, but when my mom died unexpectedly, I needed cash to cover the bills I was used to splitting with her. So, I sold it. I hoped to buy a new motorcycle sometime soon when I could afford it. Things were finally starting to even out for me, and I'd even managed to start squirreling a little away.

"I'll pick you up at six," Jason said when he dropped me off in front of the shop.

same way when he followed in our father's footsteps. What the hell were they always so secretive about?

"And I'm sure that pissed her off." I nodded. I got it. Lexie needed to feel like she came first, but Las Balas was demanding of his time. It was one of the problems that our parents had in their marriage, and they'd gotten divorced when I was eight. Jason had been ten, and it was disappointing to see him repeating our father's mistakes when he should know better.

"She'll get over it," he said confidently. "She always does."

I didn't bother to express my doubts. A person could only bend so far before they broke, and I'd hate to see that happen with Lexie. Still, they'd have to work it out on their own.

"I better go shower. I have to be at work at nine."

"I can't believe you stayed out all night when you have to work today," he commented with a slight shake of his head. "Seriously, what's the deal with that? It seems like you're never home anymore."

"I'm only twenty-three. I'm too young to spend every night cooped up at home."

I was deflecting, but he didn't call me out on it. I didn't want to get into my motives because talking about how lonely I'd been since our mom died made me feel uncomfortably vulnerable. And it depressed the hell out of me. She'd only been gone for six months, and I hadn't brought myself to even clean out her bedroom yet. This was my home, but being here alone too much made me feel like I was suffocating.

I excused myself, going to the bathroom. The first thing I did was grab a bottle of ibuprofen out of the medicine

"You know, if you're hungover, coffee's not a good idea. It'll just dehydrate you."

"What makes you think I'm hungover?" I asked, leaning against the sink while the coffee finished brewing.

"You smell like a bar."

I childishly stuck my tongue out at him. "You don't exactly smell like a daisy," I teased. "What's your excuse?"

"Just pour me a cup of coffee," he said with an eye roll.

I did, giving it to him black while I dumped a load of sugar into my own mug. I glanced at the clock on my stove. I still had over an hour before I had to be at work, so plenty of time.

"So, what was the fight about?" I asked curiously.

Jason had been living with his girlfriend for almost two years, and I thought they'd be engaged by now. They were a great fit, but I had a feeling that my brother's priorities weren't quite lined up for that ultimate commitment. Not that I had any room to talk. Thinking about and planning for the future wasn't really my thing.

"She's pissed because I have to cancel our date on Saturday."

"Isn't Saturday her birthday?"

"Yeah," he sighed and rubbed his eyes. "But Las Balas wants me to do some work for them that night. You know that I can't say no."

That was true. Jason was a prospect, which meant that he wasn't a full member until he proved himself. He basically had to do whatever they said to get in.

"What do they want you to do?"

"I can't talk about it."

I frowned. My dad had always been secretive about Las Balas's activities, but I didn't think that Jason would be the bing my shoes, I made my way toward the bar, cutting across the sand to save time.

There weren't many vehicles on the road at this early hour, so it was easy to scurry across the street once I pulled my shoes back on. My throat was dry, and there was a nasty taste in my mouth, so I hurried home to brush my teeth and take a shower before work.

When I turned onto the street my house was on, I saw that I wouldn't be able to park in my driveway. There was already a motorcycle there. It looked like Jason was at my house. Considering the early hour, I was willing to bet he spent the night. I parked at the curb and entered the house. The first thing I saw was my brother sleeping on my couch, snoring loudly. I didn't bother to be quiet as I closed the door behind me, and he jolted awake.

"Where the hell have you been?" he asked through a yawn as he blinked at me sleepily. His thick black hair was a mess, and there was a red mark on the side of his face from where it had been pressed against the arm of the couch.

"You're not my keeper," I said, tossing my purse onto the small table by the door. "The question is, why are you in my house?"

I walked past him into the kitchen and turned on the coffee maker. Within seconds, the heavenly smell of caffeinated brew filled the small kitchen.

"Me and Lexie had a fight, so I crashed here," he explained, following me and plopping down at the kitchen table.

"You didn't think to *ask*?"

He shrugged carelessly. "I know where you keep the spare key. Besides, you weren't even home."

I would've come home if I'd known he was here, but I didn't tell him that.

Not long after that, I left the bar, finding that it wasn't nearly as fun without someone I knew to talk to. The sensible thing would have been to go home, even if I had to order an Uber because of the drinking, but I didn't want to do that. Instead, I crossed the street, heading for the beach.

In the light of day, even with a throbbing hangover headache, I could see that wandering off by myself in the middle of the night after drinking heavily wasn't the best idea. I carried mace on my keyring, but that didn't mean I was invincible.

Once I reached the sand, I had pulled off my shoes and socks so that I could walk along the edge of the water barefoot. The gentle waves ran over my feet, wetting the bottom of the legs of my skinny jeans, and my toes sank into the wet sand with each step.

I wasn't sure how long I had walked the beach before deciding to stop and rest. I had just intended to sit for a moment before heading back toward my car, hoping that I would be sober enough to drive home by the time I got there. But I made the mistake of lying back on the white sand, gazing at the sky above, trying to find shapes in the stars.

The next thing I knew, a damn seagull woke me up.

Sitting up, I used my hand to block the sun from my eyes as I looked around. I could tell that it was early by the positioning of the sun, which was good because I didn't need to be late for work two days in a row.

I craned my neck and saw that I hadn't walked nearly as far as I thought I had last night. My car was still sitting in the bar's parking lot. I got to my feet, seeing that every inch of my clothing was covered in sand. I brushed it off as well as I could, going as far as to shake out my long hair before pulling it up with a hair tie that was around my wrist. Grab-

THREE
KAT

I woke up to the sound of seagulls squawking. Despite this, my location didn't register in my brain right away. The pounding ache in my head stole all my attention, and I groaned before I even opened my eyes. My arm was thrown across my face, covering my eyes, and I knew the meaning of regret as I moved it away.

The newly risen sun was already shining too brightly, hurting my eyes even through my closed lids. I realized I was outside, and the events of last night came back to me.

Piper and I had gone to the Copper Bar, where I was quick to dump money into the jukebox and pick enough music to last for two hours. We drank, gladly accepting free drinks from men in the bar without offering anything in return other than polite conversation, and danced the night away.

None of the men in the place caught my eye, but Piper was a different story. Around midnight, she told me that she was leaving, and the guy on her arm looked startlingly like Nicholas Cage.

Good for her, I guess.

Printed in Great Britain
by Amazon

TWENTY
BLADE

"That's one sweet-ass ride, man," I turned toward the voice speaking and saw a group of four men standing on the edge of the Blue Dog's parking lot. They were all smoking joints and looked like biker wannabes. They were too *clean* with their perfectly trimmed fingernails and leather jackets that looked like they just came off the hanger at the store.

"Thanks," I said with a nod, but I didn't stop to talk.

Walking into the bar, I waited for a second for my eyes to adjust before looking around. Trainer was sitting in his usual spot at the bar, while Hawk and Pin played a game of pool in the back. It looked like they both sucked, but half of their attention was on a college football game on the flat screens hanging around the bar.

The only other person in the place was Axel, who was behind the bar. I took a seat next to Trainer, and Axel handed over a beer before I even had to ask.

"What's up?" I asked Trainer as I shrugged out of my jacket.

"Taking Eve on a date tonight," he shrugged. "Little time out of the house without the kids."

"Nice."

"It would be nicer if she'd let Swole keep the kids overnight."

I laughed. Poor guy must have been sex-deprived since the baby came along. "Why won't she?"

"She says Ashley is too little to be away from us overnight."

"At three months old? She must be crazy. That girl should have her own place by now."

Trainer punched me in the arm. I thought it was meant to be playful, but the guy was so damn big that he couldn't seem to help packing a wallop.

"You know I'm crazy about my baby girl, but I want a night with my wife."

"That's a bummer," I said. I really didn't have any pearls of wisdom for the guy. I had never spent much time around kids and had no intention of having my own.

"Gee, thanks. What about you? What are you up to tonight?"

I lifted my beer bottle and gave him a wry grin. "Just a whole lot of this."

"Now, *that's* the bummer."

I shrugged. I was just glad that it wasn't my turn to go walk around with a metal detector for three hours. That was probably why the bar was so empty on a Friday evening. We'd probably get some townies in later, mostly women looking for a good time. I didn't see myself picking any of them up, though. I couldn't get my stupid mind off Kat long enough to take anyone else to bed.

The door of the bar opened again, and I glanced over to see the four men from the parking lot enter. The smell of pot clung to them, and they were all downright giddy.

"What's up, boys?" the same man that had addressed

me asked the room at large as the four of them took a table near the jukebox.

None of us answered directly. We just watched him as he approached the bar.

"Four of your finest domestic brews for me and my buddies," the man said, slapping a fifty-dollar bill on the bar.

Ah, that made sense. This guy was probably from Fletcher Pointe, a wealthy town just to the east of La Playa. We got people like this in here sometimes, rich guys that wanted to play like they were tough guys. They had romanticized the biker life, or maybe they thought it would get them women, and the ultimate way of showing off was to come to a *real* biker bar, to fraternize with the Outlaw Souls as if they belonged. People like this were generally harmless and occasionally amusing.

"Hammond Boothe," the guy said, holding his hand out to me.

Hammond?

Even this guy's name was showy.

"Blade," I said, squeezing his fingers as I shook his hand.

"Blade...*nice*. Did you get to pick your own nickname?"

"What makes you think it's a nickname?" I asked.

"Well..." he trailed off with nervous laughter as he looked as Axel, then back to me. "I mean... Blade isn't a real name."

"But Hammond is?"

Trainer barked out a loud laugh, making Hammond jump before giving us a smile of his own.

"Fair enough. You guys are Outlaw Souls, right?"

"Maybe," I said noncommittally. "And what are you guys?"

Hammond looked back over at his friends, then at me.

"Just a couple of guys that like riding. Thought you guys might be cool."

"Oh, we're very cool," I said. "But if you want to hang out here, you'll have to prove yourself."

Axel grinned broadly as he realized what I was doing.

"How?" Hammond asked.

"Taking on a *real* biker in a drinking contest."

"I can do that," Hammond said confidently.

"We put money on the line. Five hundred."

He didn't even hesitate. "Done."

"You heard the man Axel. Set us up with Jameson."

"Whoa," Hammond said, looking uncertain. "Whisky? That's some hard shit."

"You wanna back out?" I asked with a challenge in my voice. I made sure it was loud enough for his buddies to hear.

"No way," Hammond said, literally puffing out his chest.

"Let's do it then."

I turned to Trainer with a grin and saw laughter in his eyes. It looked like I had found some fun for my Friday night, after all. Axel poured the drinks and carried them to the table, and Hammond's eyes widened when he saw how much there was. This was going to be like taking candy from a baby.

THE NEXT DAY, I was five hundred dollars richer, but I was also hungover. The tattoo shop seemed a thousand times brighter than usual, and I wasn't in the mood for work. But here I was, wearing sunglasses inside and lounging in my tattoo chair. I didn't have an appointment for another hour, so I figured I might as well make use of the thing.

"Rough night?" Kat's voice was definitely louder than usual, and I had an idea that she was doing that on purpose.

"Can you lower your voice to foghorn level, please?" I asked. Piper snickered nearby.

"You know what I think, Piper?" Kat said, tapping her chin thoughtfully. "I think I'll have the triple bacon cheeseburger from the food truck down the street for lunch. You know, the really greasy one? And fries with dripping cheese sauce."

My stomach rolled.

"You're the worst," I groaned.

She just laughed. That sound shouldn't make me feel so light.

I gathered my willpower to get up out of the chair, knowing that I should try to start getting ready for my appointment soon. I groaned as my temples throbbed.

"Here," Kat said. When I turned her way, I saw that she was holding out two red pills in her hand. "It's ibuprofen."

"Thanks." I took the pills dry, but she handed me a bottle of water too. I drained it.

By the time my client arrived, I felt so much better. I would think that Kat was a saint if she wasn't constantly sending me mixed signals. She was so damn hot and cold, but all I wanted was to fuck her again.

I managed to eat some beef jerky in the afternoon without my stomach rebelling, so I felt damn near normal by the end of the day. I told myself firmly that I was *not* doing drinking contests anymore.

Either that, or next time, I was going to put more money on the line.

When it was time to leave for the day, Piper left before

Kat and I were done cleaning. It was the first time I'd been in this space with her alone since our first kiss. It felt like a lifetime ago, but I couldn't help thinking about it. *Wanting* it.

"Kat," I said, stopping her just as she was about to leave.

"What?" she asked, but when she turned to face me, I could see that her breath had quickened. She knew what I was thinking, and I hoped she was thinking the same thing.

I moved closer to her until only a few feet separated us.

"I have an idea."

"Oh, really?" she furrowed an eyebrow. "And what's that?"

"A...chemistry experiment, of sorts."

"What are you talking about?"

"Sex, Kat," I stepped closer so that we were almost touching. So close, but not quite there. "I'm talking about taking you to my apartment and spreading you wide."

She visibly shuddered, but her gaze dropped to the floor. "I told you, Blade. We can't. Las Balas and Outlaw Souls are—"

"That doesn't matter. Not if it's just sex."

"No strings attached?" she asked with a sexy little smile.

"Exactly," I agreed.

"Well...as long as we're in agreement, I don't see why we couldn't do that."

My cock was heavy in my pants, and I desperately wanted to take her right here, but that wasn't an option.

"Follow me back to my place."

"Now?" she asked with wide eyes.

"Fuck yeah."

We started to leave when something else occurred to me. "Wait a minute, if we're going to do this, I have one condition."

"What's that?" she asked suspiciously.

"I get to call you Kitten whenever I want."

"Fine," she agreed, much easier than I expected. "Now, let's get the hell out of here."

Anticipation curled in my stomach. I could hardly wait.

TWENTY-ONE
KAT

I pulled my jeans on while Blade laid in bed, wearing only a pair of boxers. We'd settled into this no-strings-attached sexual relationship over the last few days, and it was working well. I tried to keep some distance between us at work, but after hours, I went to his place for a couple of rounds between the sheets. I never stayed the night, though, and Blade didn't ask.

Today was a Saturday, which meant that I wasn't supposed to see him at all, but he'd sent me a text message in the morning, offering some afternoon delight that I couldn't pass up. I scanned the room, looking for my shirt.

"Where are you going?" Blade asked, watching me.

I finally spotted my tank top hanging off the lampshade. I grabbed it, pulling it over my head.

"I want to go shopping around for a bike."

"A motorcycle?" he asked, sitting up in bed.

"No, a bicycle," I said, my voice dripping with sarcasm.

"Okay, smartass."

"I'll see you later." I picked up my boots from the floor, heading for the exit.

"I could help you."

I stopped walking and turned to look at him. "What?"

Blade got off the bed and picked up his jeans from the floor. "I can help you get a bike."

I narrowed my eyes at him suspiciously. "Why would you do that?"

"Uh, to be *nice*?"

I frowned. "You don't have to do that. We're not a couple."

Blade rolled his eyes. "I don't have to be dating you to be a nice guy."

"Says the Outlaw Soul."

"Just come with me," he said impatiently. I sat down on the edge of the bed and pulled my boots on.

"Fine. Where are we going?"

"To see a friend of mine. He fixes up bikes and sells them."

"This *friend* have a name?"

"Trainer."

I didn't recognize the name. "Not a member of your club, I hope."

Blade didn't respond, just kept getting dressed, which really told me all that I needed to know.

"Nope," I stood, shaking my head. "No way."

"Grow up, Kat," Blade's use of my name stopped me short. I was so used to him calling me Kitten, whether I wanted him to or not, that it felt weird to hear my name come out of his mouth instead. He let out a sigh while I stared at him. "It's a bike purchase. A business transaction. It has nothing to do with my club versus your club. It doesn't mean anything, just like our sexual relationship."

I struggled not to wince as he threw my words right

back at me. They sounded so damn cold when on the receiving end.

"Fine, but if he's a creep, I'm never going to let you forget it."

"Of course you won't," he agreed, and I spotted a hint of a smile on his face.

I followed him out the door of his apartment and down the stairs to the parking lot. "You know, Outlaw Souls owns an apartment complex. I'll probably be moving into it once my lease is up here."

"When is that?" I asked.

"Six months."

At least I had time to figure out a different place to meet up with him. Obviously, I wouldn't go to the new apartment, and I didn't want him at my home. It made it too personal for me, especially now that I was redecorating the place and making it my own. Even more than that, I didn't want Blade in my bed again because that was where we had sex for the first time before everything between us went to shit.

It occurred to me that I was thinking way too long-term here. If this was really just a casual sex situation, then it probably wouldn't still be happening in six months.

Something within me somersaulted at that thought, but I ignored it.

Hopping onto the back of Blade's bike, I wrapped my arms around him, trying not to think too much about how comfortable I was here. He rode along the back roads, which he had told me were more fun to ride than straightaways. I wasn't sure where we were going until we pulled up in front of Ortega Auto. I'd never been here before, of course, but I knew it to be the property of Outlaw Souls.

"Damn it, Blade. Why did you have to bring me here?" I

asked, whipping the helmet off of my head. I slapped his back with the palm of my hand, but it was like hitting a wall.

"This is where the bike is," he said, exasperated.

I hopped off the back of the bike, looking around. I didn't spot anyone else nearby, but I couldn't shake my discomfort. This was not somewhere that I should be.

Yet, I didn't feel like I was actually in danger. Maybe that was foolish. I'd seen how my dad and others put the motorcycle club above everyone else, but I was sure that Blade would never allow me to come to harm.

"Come on," he said, walking toward a side door.

I fell into step behind him. I didn't like that he'd brought me here, but I supposed that I owed him a chance. *This bike better be great.*

There was nothing special about the interior of the garage. It could have been any other auto shop in the country with its stained concrete floors, big red toolboxes all over the place, and the smell of oil in the air. I knew where we were going without being told. There were a few cars in the bays, but only one bike in sight. I recognized it as a Harley Street 750. It was small, one of the smallest options in that brand, which would be good for me since I was a little on the short side. I needed something small enough to allow my feet to touch the ground while straddling it.

Blade and I approached the bike side-by-side, and I ran my eyes over it. It was pretty with its burnt orange paint color on the tank and black leather saddlebags. But, I'd have to see how it rode before getting too excited.

A large man came out of the office near the back of the shop, wiping his hands on a dirty red rag. With a full beard and long hair, he had a distinctive look, and I could imagine that some people would find him intimidating, but I didn't.

I'd had some big men in my chair and knew that things like size and facial hair didn't really have anything to do with being tough. Sometimes, the scariest looking men cried while I used my tattoo gun on them.

Blade stepped forward and clasped hands with the man, and they patted each other's backs. It was such a cute *bro* greeting that I couldn't help but smile.

"Kat, this is Trainer," Blade said as they came over to me. "He's a whiz with these bikes, and I've asked him to give you a good deal."

I shook Trainer's hand and listened to his rundown of the bike. He really knew his stuff, covering everything from the type of engine to the power, to fuel return and cooling system. It was a lot of technical stuff that I didn't necessarily care about, but it did instill confidence in me that he knew what he was talking about.

Trainer opened one of the bay doors and let me take it out into the parking lot for a test drive, and I loved how nimble it was. The bike itself wasn't too heavy for my small frame to handle, and I loved the little windshield he'd installed. My last bike didn't have one.

I had brought along my savings, pulled straight from the shoebox and tucked into my boot for safe-keeping. I had managed to add to it in the last couple of weeks enough to reach five thousand dollars. I knew that wasn't a lot of money and Trainer could probably get more out of this bike, so I was a bundle of nerves when I parked it back inside the garage and hopped off the talk about purchasing the motorcycle.

Trainer admitted that he got the bike for a steal and had only put a couple thousand dollars into it. He was planning to ask six thousand for it, but to my shock, he easily accepted the five that I had on me. I couldn't believe my luck and decided that Trainer wasn't so bad, for an Outlaw Soul.

"I told you I could help you," Blade said smugly after I had exchanged the cash for the keys and Trainer had gone back into the office, probably to put that cash in a safe.

"Yeah, yeah," I said dismissively, but I grinned like an idiot as I mounted my new bike. I really loved it. "I can't wait to take this thing out of the parking lot. It's been too long since I went on a ride."

"I'll come with you," Blade said.

I wanted to say no. We were already spending too much time together, breaking my *no strings attached* rule. But he was the reason that I had this new bike. I felt like I owed him, and all he wanted was to ride in formation together.

"Fine," I said, "but I'm leading. Non-negotiable."

"No problem. I like the view from behind anyway."

"Pig."

He playfully oinked in my direction before jogging over to his own bike. I didn't wait for him to get his helmet on and mount his bike. I was sure he'd catch up. So, I shifted into gear and twisted the throttle, leading the bike out of the parking lot. There wasn't a ton of traffic on this street, which I was sure appealed to Outlaw Souls when they obtained this building, so I didn't have to wait at all before pulling out onto the road.

The wind whipped around me as I sped up, shifting into a higher gear. I felt powerful and free like this, and the bike was like an extension of my own body. It was so easy to control.

It took no time at all for Blade to catch up to me, falling into formation by riding behind me in the other side of the lane. We'd only ever be side-by-side during stops at stop signs or traffic lights. It had been a while since I rode, but it all came back to me easily. I found that I was operating the motorcycle without even thinking about it. It was like my body remembered what to do without the need for input from my brain.

I didn't have a destination in mind. I just wanted to *go*. So, I wound my way through La Playa randomly, traveling familiar roads. I wasn't thinking.

Then, I passed a trio of riders going in the opposite direction. I immediately recognized the lead rider as my dad. Dread crept up my spine, and I pulled off the road right after they passed. What if my dad recognized me? It might not be likely because I was wearing a full-face helmet, but it was possible. I looked over at Blade as he pulled up alongside me.

Shit.

Damn Blade and the stupid patch he was wearing on the back of his jacket. If my dad recognized me *and* saw that, it was going to cause a problem.

"What's wrong?" Blade asked as he pulled off his helmet. "Why'd we stop?"

"That was my dad we passed. *Fuck.*"

"So?"

"*So?*" I repeated, shaking my head. "Look at what you're wearing."

Blade frowned. "Is this another Outlaw Souls thing?"

"Of course it is. My relationship with him is rocky enough without him thinking that I'm involved with Outlaw Souls."

"You know what? That's pretty fucking sad if you ask me. Why should you have to worry about what he thinks? What's he done to deserve such devotion?"

"He's my dad," I said defensively. I didn't want him to know that he made a good point. It didn't change anything.

"Yeah, well, dad's aren't always all they're cracked up to be."

"It's called loyalty, Blade. Maybe they don't care about that in Outlaw Souls, but Las Balas takes that seriously."

"Whatever, Kat." Blade looked pissed, and I hated that it bothered me. "I'm out of here."

I watched him ride away, trying not to feel too guilty. I knew that I'd hurt his feelings, but I knew my dad would be angry if I were fraternizing with the enemy. When Blade was out of sight, I pulled my helmet back on and pointed my new bike toward home. Somehow, the thrill of the ride had left me.

TWENTY-TWO
BLADE

I was back at Luca's street fighting ring. I knew it was a back idea, with Outlaw Souls trying to find the weapons and force him out of town. Also, I hadn't harassed Raymond Groves's widow the way that Luca asked me to. I wasn't sure how I would talk my way out of that.

But I always went a little nuts on the anniversary of my brother's death, which happened to be today. For some reason, knowing that it happened on this date brought all the dark shit I tried to keep buried right to the surface.

I needed an outlet, and fighting was as good as it got. Of course, I'd used sex as a distraction in the past, but my relationship with Kat was complicated—if I could even call it a relationship at all—and I wasn't interested in sleeping with anyone else. I supposed that I *could* since we'd agreed to have emotionless, casual sex, but I hadn't found anyone else attractive since that first night I spent with her. She was too good in bed.

Shockingly, luck was on my side tonight, and Luca was absent again. I had no idea what he was up to, but I didn't care. I was just happy that I didn't have to act like I was interested in getting paid to do his dirty work. I wasn't sure I had it in me to even pretend tonight.

Alex was also absent, but that was because I didn't invite him. He was my cousin, so he knew exactly what today was, and I didn't want to have to see his pity-filled gaze. He'd probably try to get me to talk about my feelings too.

No, thank you.

I had already participated in one fight this evening, and my opponent was a tough motherfucker. I'd won in the end, pummeling his face a couple more times than I needed to as a way to release some aggression, but I'd also taken a knee to the kidneys and was surely sporting a black eye.

It didn't matter. Nothing mattered. The world was full of bad shit, and life tended to screw you over at any opportunity.

I closed my eyes and steadied my breathing as I waited for the current fight to end so that I could go another round. I never did that, always signing up for one match and getting the hell out of here, but I was looking to hurt someone tonight. Or maybe I wanted to get hurt.

I didn't know anymore.

When it was time to step back into the ring, I knew that my focus was off, but I didn't care. My opponent for this fight was young. He almost looked like a teenager, but he was muscular. When the fight began, we started circling each other. I'd seen my opponent fight, and I knew that his style was similar to my own—keep moving. This should be interesting.

I surged forward, ready to jab him in his exposed side, but he pivoted at the last second, using my own momentum against me to kick at my leg, making contact that sent me sprawling.

It didn't feel good to land on the concrete, but I popped right back up, turning back to face the guy. I saw red when he shot me a cocky smirk. Trying to channel that anger into the fight, I came at him again. I anticipated his defensive move this time and managed to misdirect him and swipe his legs. He landed much harder than I had, but he didn't take even a second to recover. Instead, he threw himself into me, taking me down to the ground with a bear hug around my waist.

Suddenly the fight turned into a wrestling match, and that wasn't my strong suit. I preferred to keep my distance as much as possible. Still, I tried my best to overpower him, ignoring the way the bare skin of my back burned from scraping against the rough concrete beneath us.

He hooked his arm around my neck, and I head-butted him to loosen his grip before I lost too much oxygen and passed out. Rolling over, I tried to pin him beneath me, but his fist collided with my jaw, and the next thing I knew, he was on top of me. I kept my arms up, trying to block my face from his blows, but he managed to get one past. I saw stars as he hit me in the side of the head, and my right temple throbbed.

Shit. I was in trouble here.

I brought my legs up, trying to knock him off of me, but it didn't work, so I bucked like a bronco and was able to unseat him. I had a brief moment of satisfaction as I started to stand. I made it onto my hands and knees before his leg swung around, catching me in the ribs. I heard a sickening crack as pain exploded in my side. My strength left me, and I collapsed onto the floor.

It was the strangest thing, but I didn't mind losing this fight. As my opponent stood above me, I only cared about the adrenaline rush that flooded my system, making me feel alive. That was all I wanted today, to feel something other than regret and grief.

Coming here might have been reckless, but it was worth it.

I KNOCKED on the door of Kat's house, telling myself that I was an idiot for coming here. I knew that she didn't want to fuck at her place. I wasn't clear on the reason for it, but I suspected it was just another attempt to keep me at a distance. I should probably take a hint.

Instead, I'd come here after leaving the warehouse. I'd picked myself up off the floor after my second fight, using my t-shirt to wipe the sweat and blood from my face before shrugging on my jacket over my bare torso.

The door of the house opened and revealed Kat in a thin white t-shirt with no bra underneath and a pair of skimpy shorts. Her legs were long and smooth, and I trailed my eyes all the way down to her black toenails. Her toes curled as I looked at them, making me smile. She folded her arms across her chest and leaned her shoulder against the doorframe as she looked at me through the screen door.

"You look like shit," she said, and I grinned. I knew that I looked like a walking bruise, but I couldn't bring myself to care. I'd heal.

"And you're such a charmer."

"What are you doing here?"

I shrugged. I really didn't have a good answer for that. I wasn't here for sex. As good as it was, tonight wasn't a good time for that. My emotions were already fucked.

"Can I come in?" I asked.

She hesitated, staring at me for a long moment. I wasn't

sure what she saw in my eyes, but it must have convinced her because she nodded and stepped back. I opened the screen door and entered the house. It looked different than the last time I was here, on the night of our first date.

"You redecorating?" I asked, looking around. I had been pretty damn distracted that night, but the following morning, I remembered thinking that the place didn't really feel like Kat. It made sense when she told me that her mom used to live with her. There were a lot of floral patterns and old furniture. Now, there was a more modern feeling to the place. The walls were dark, but the furniture and décor were light and bright. Somehow, it screamed *Kat*.

"Yeah. Been working on it for a couple of weeks. It was time."

I didn't hear the sadness in her voice that I would have expected, and I was happy for her. She was finally moving on from her mom's death. I wish I was that strong. My life kept moving forward, but I still felt haunted by Mark after all these years. Maybe I always would.

"You want a beer?" she asked.

"If I ever say no to that question, there's something seriously wrong."

She gifted me with a small half-smile before going into the kitchen and grabbing two beers from the fridge. She twisted the tops off and threw them into the garbage before handing mine over.

"I was just about to go sit outside for a bit," she said, walking toward the back door. From behind, her shorts were so short that I could see the bottoms of her ass cheeks. I took a big gulp of my cold beer, rethinking whether I was in a good headspace for sex tonight. Why did she have to be so irresistible?

Kat looked back at me over her shoulder. "You coming?"

I followed her outside, where there was a covered patio. A glass-topped table was surrounded by cushioned patio chairs sitting next to a propane grill. Kat took a seat, and I sat across from her. Kat lit a citronella candle, and the scent of it filled the air between us.

"What's going on, Blade?" she asked after we'd been sitting in silence together for several minutes. I was comfortable with it, but I should have known that Kat would question me. I was lucky that she let me in the house at all.

I sighed before tipping my beer bottle back and emptying it. I stood.

"I'm gonna grab another. You want one?"

"Sure."

I took my time in the house, but when I returned, Kat was waiting patiently. She wasn't going to let me get out of answering her question. I knew she had a right to know what was up with me, but it was hard to talk about. After I resumed my seat, I leaned forward, resting my elbows on the table.

"My brother Mark died ten years ago today."

"Holy shit," Kat said after a moment. "I'm so sorry."

"Yeah, well..." I didn't know what to say. Her words were meant to comfort, but I'd realized long ago that there was nothing that could make this better.

"Can I ask what happened?"

"Yeah," I stared at the label of my beer bottle without really seeing it. "He killed himself."

I didn't look up at Kat's sharp intake of breath. I didn't want to see her feeling sorry for me.

"I was sixteen. Mark was my older brother, but only by two years, so we were always pretty close." I rubbed my eyes, trying to somehow scrub away the image in my mind. It wouldn't work. It never did. "I found him afterward."

"You...oh, my god, Blade."

"Yeah," I nodded. "It was an overdose."

"You're sure it was intentional?"

"Definitely. He took an entire bottle of his antidepressants. He didn't leave a note or anything, but it was pretty clear that he meant to do it."

I clenched my fists as the familiar helpless anger flooded me. I hated being angry at Mark, but every time I thought about him leaving me behind like that...I just couldn't help it.

"I'd be angry, too," Kat said, her voice soft. It felt like she was reading my mind, and a part of me resented her for it, but that wasn't fair.

"I shouldn't be," I shook my head. "I know that's selfish of me, but damn it, he was my only friend. We moved all over the damn place growing up since our dad was in the army. He knew he was all I had."

I hadn't talked about this with anyone, not even the therapist that my mom had made me see after Mark's death. I wasn't sure why I was opening up to Kat now. She was still trying to keep me at arm's length, convinced that we should be enemies.

"So, he struggled with depression?"

"For years. Our dad's a real hard-ass and had all these expectations for the two of us, but especially Mark. He was the golden child. So, he tried to hide his depression for a long time. When he turned eighteen, he got on medication without our old man knowing. I thought it was working, but...clearly, I was wrong."

"You know that's not your fault, right?"

I let out a humorless chuckle. "Are you reading my mind or something?"

"No, but I think I've gotten to know you pretty well over the last few weeks."

"Despite your best efforts."

"That's not fair," she said.

I drained my second beer. "Haven't you been listening? Life's not fair."

"I'm going to bed," she said, rising. She started to walk past me, but I reached out and grabbed hold of her wrist.

"I'm sorry," I said, not even sure what I was apologizing for. I just didn't want her to make me leave. Just for tonight, I wanted to act like Kat gave a crap about me, that I was more to her than just sex.

Turning her hand over, Kat pulled me to my feet. "Come to bed."

I wasn't going to question it. Blowing out the candle, I followed her into the house and down the hall to her bedroom. I didn't realize how tired I was until I sat on her bed to take my boots off. I felt like I could just collapse onto the comfortable mattress. I unzipped my jacket and felt Kat's eyes on me.

"You're not wearing a shirt? What kind of a fashion statement are you trying to make?"

"It was dirty after my fight," I explained, tossing the jacket onto an easy chair in the corner.

"Fight? So, that's why you look like you've been beaten with a bat."

"Street fighting. I wanted to let out some aggression."

"Looks like you lost."

I kicked off my jeans so that I was just wearing a pair of boxers. Kat pulled back the sheets and slid into bed. When I did the same, she moved closer, pressing herself into my side and resting her head on my shoulder. I told myself not to read too much into it. She just felt sorry for me, and things between us would return to normal in the light of day. But it still felt really good.

I turned off the lamp on the table beside me, leaving us in almost total darkness. I couldn't see Kat, but I could feel her and hear her even breathing. I felt my eyelids grow heavier and was almost asleep when her voice spoke, pulling me away from sleep.

"You know, it's weird. Our dads are complete opposites. Yours is an intense army man with all these expectations, while mine is a drunk that probably doesn't think about me at all."

"That can't be true," I said, even though the man was a Las Balas member. How could he not care about someone like Kat?

"It is. Sometimes I wish that we were closer, but I'm not going to spend my life trying to establish a relationship with someone that doesn't care enough to try."

"Fuck him," I said, once again struggling to stay awake. I wanted to talk to her while I could. She'd be back to pushing me away soon. But exhaustion was winning the fight.

"I wish it was that easy."

Me too. That was my last thought before I finally surrendered to sleep.

KAT WAS ALREADY AWAKE and showered when I stumbled out of her bedroom the following morning. I found her in the living room, scrolling through television channels.

"You have any Tylenol around here?" I asked, taking a seat on the other end of the couch. I didn't even have to speak to her to know that her walls were back up. She'd sent the message by leaving me to sleep in her bed by myself.

"In the bathroom," she said without looking away from the TV screen.

I sighed through my nose and stood, walking to the bathroom and rummaging through the medicine cabinet. I needed something to take the edge off the aches and pains from my losing the fight last night.

I went back into the bedroom instead of joining Kat in the living room. I pulled on my jeans and boots, carrying my jacket into the kitchen, where I put it on the back of a chair at the table. I poured myself a pot of coffee and looked out the window above the sink, where a familiar motorcycle was pulling into the driveway beside my own.

"Your brother's here," I told Kat. She clicked off the television and joined me at the sink.

"What is he doing here?" she mumbled to herself.

She didn't look happy, and I had a pretty good idea that it was because I was here.

"I guess I'll go," I said, putting my half-empty mug into the sink. "Thanks for not turning me away last night."

Kat finally looked directly at me, and her expression softened. "I really am sorry to hear about your brother."

The front door opened, and Kat turned away from me. I felt somehow colder without her attention.

"Hey, Kat, the place looks great," Jason said as he walked in and looked around. "You've really—"

He stopped speaking as he turned and saw me standing shirtless in the kitchen. His mouth opened and closed for a moment, and he looked like a fish out of water.

"This is Blade," Kat said unenthusiastically. "We work together."

"Work, huh? Is that what they call it these days?"

Jason's wide grin was teasing, and I could see the affection between the two of them. I didn't want to intrude on it if Kat didn't want me here, and she clearly didn't.

"I'll head out," I said, grabbing my jacket off the kitchen chair and pulling it on. "Let you guys have some time alone."

I'd only made it three steps when Jason's voice lashed out, no longer good-humored. "What the fuck is that?"

I stopped and glanced over my shoulder to see his eyes glued to the back of my jacket, to my Outlaw Souls patch.

"Do we have a problem here?" I asked, trying not to sound too confrontational. I knew that this was exactly what Kat was worried about happening.

"Hell yeah. We do." He stepped closer, coming up into my face. "What the fuck is an Outlaw Soul doing at my sister's house? Do you think you're going to get to us through her?"

"Absolutely not," I said firmly, looking at Kat to make sure that she didn't think that. I was frustrated when I couldn't read her face.

Jason followed my gaze, looking at Kat in shock. "You're fucking this guy?"

"Watch it," I snapped, not liking the tone he was using with her.

"Just go, Blade," Kat said, folding her arms across her chest as she leveled a glare at her brother. I could have sworn that he faltered at the sight of it.

I smirked. I should have known that she could handle herself against him.

"See you at work tomorrow," I replied.

It was time to get the hell out of there.

TWENTY-THREE

KAT

"Are you fucking kidding me?" Jason asked incredulously the second that Blade was out of the door.

"It's none of your business, Jason," I told him.

"What are you doing, Kat? He's an Outlaw Soul. You know that they have a vendetta against Las Balas. Last year, they gave Rage's girl a hell of a hard time."

"Why?"

"I'm not supposed to talk about it," he said, and I saw something shifty in his eyes. There was more to the story that he wasn't going to share.

"Then, it's not a good example. Don't worry about Blade. He knows I'm loyal to Las Balas."

"Are you sure about that? What happens as you two keep dating? Are you going to fall for this guy and betray us?"

"Fuck you, Jason," I spat bitterly.

Guilt flashed across his face. He knew he'd gone too far.

"You know that I'd never do that, not that I even could. I don't know jack shit about what you guys get up to."

Jason seemed to deflate on a sigh. He walked over to the kitchen table and pulled out a chair before sinking into it.

"I know. I'm just worried."

"I can take care of myself. I think you know that."

"Yeah, I do," he agreed. "But *why*? Why would you date an Outlaw Soul in the first place?"

"I'm not dating him," I insisted. I wasn't sure what the hell we were doing anymore, but this situation was exactly why we couldn't work as a couple. A line had been drawn in the sand long before we met, and the two of us were on opposite sides.

"Could've fooled me."

"Haven't you ever heard of casual sex?"

"Ew," he scrunched his nose.

"Oh, grow up," I said, sitting down next to him. "The point is that I know the two of us can't work together. So, we fuck with no emotional attachment."

Jason seemed to relax. "Does *he* know that? Because he seemed a little...*protective*."

"Yes, he knows. Don't worry about it."

My tone made it clear that the topic was closed for discussion. Jason put his hands up defensively. "Okay, fine."

"What are you doing here, anyway?" I asked.

Jason's entire demeanor changed. A wide smile stretched across his face, and he sat up straighter, with a spark in his eyes.

"I came to share the good news. Lexie's pregnant."

I let out a happy squeal and threw my arms around his neck. "Oh my god. That's amazing."

"Can you believe it? I'm going to be a dad."

At those words, I felt a sliver of dread. Even though I had just been proclaiming loyalty to Las Balas, I didn't want Jason to continue with his pursuit of membership now that he had a child on the way. History had a way of repeating itself, and I didn't want Jason to choose Las Balas over his family the way that our dad did. But I couldn't tell him that. I knew him, and he'd just assure me that I was overreacting. So, I just kept smiling and hugged him tighter.

"I'M GOING TO BE AN AUNTIE," I told Piper happily as soon as she walked into the tattoo shop the next day.

"What?" she blinked, startled. Okay, maybe I went a little supersonic.

"Jason's having a baby. Lexie's pregnant."

"Wow. That's awesome," Piper said as she walked into her workstation and set down the big tote bag that she liked to use as a purse.

"Right? She's only eight weeks along, so there's still a ton of time, but he's already talking about teaching his son to ride a bike."

"Let me guess, you don't mean a bicycle?"

"Nope," I shook my head. "Motorcycle all the way."

Piper snickered. "He's so crazy."

"What if it's a girl?" Blade asked from his work station. I gave him a withering look for butting in but decided to answer. I was in too good of a mood to be mean to Blade right now.

"I'll teach her that girls can ride too, of course."

"Will he be happy if it's a girl, though?" Piper asked.

"I'm sure he will. He pictures a little boy because he thinks a boy will be easier to relate to, but if it's a girl that looks just like Lexie? Come on, she'll have him wrapped around her little finger."

Piper sighed with a dreamy look on her face.

"I can't wait to have kids," she said wistfully.

"Why don't you do it now?" Blade asked. "What are you waiting for?"

"A man that also wants kids would be nice."

"Yeah, make sure he wants them," Blade said. "Some guys just aren't cut out for it."

"Like you?" I asked curiously, despite myself.

"For sure. I'm not the dad type. Cool uncle? Sure. But no, I don't want to be a dad."

I didn't say anything in response, but Piper looked back and forth between the two of us for a moment before speaking for me.

"Kat doesn't want kids either."

"You don't?" Blade asked.

"No."

My reply was short. I was trying not to engage with Blade too much. After my conversation with Jason yesterday reminded me why I wasn't dating him, I told myself to do a better job at keeping him at arm's length. I should probably stop having sex with him, too, but that was going to be hard. I found that our physical activities scratched an itch that I couldn't stand to leave unattended again.

"She also doesn't believe in marriage," Piper said.

"Thank you, *Piper*," I snapped impatiently. "And I *believe* in it. I know it exists. I just don't think it's for everyone."

"It's not for *you*, you mean." Blade sounded way too interested in this topic. I didn't like it. My future was none of his concern.

"You know what? I have a client coming in here in ten minutes, and I have to free draw a unicorn for her. So, I'm going to work on that," I said, turning my back to both of them as I started working on the drawing, making it clear that I didn't want to talk about this any longer.

"You know, Blade. Marriage is just a piece of paper. I think that Kat values a more significant commitment than that. You know, a man that sticks around."

"I can hear you," I said. Come on, I was still sitting right here.

"Of course, you can," Piper agreed, and Blade chuckled.

I rolled my eyes and focused on work. I knew that my best friend was just trying to help me be happy, but she had to get this idea of helping Blade and me get together out of her head. They both did.

TWENTY-FOUR

BLADE

Over the past week, every member of the Outlaw Souls motorcycle club had spent hours scouring Raymond Groves's property just outside La Playa with a metal detector. It wasn't a bad gig, walking around in nature, but now it was time to dig.

This part sucked.

There was no way of knowing how deep the weapons were buried, so using some kind of equipment wasn't an option. We might damage what was there, or set it off if there was anything like hand grenades in the stash.

So, it was all hands on deck as we all took a shovel. There were only three spots left on the entire property that had been marked with a red X after Hawk determined that there was an old steel water line that ran right through the property. We had all run across it at least once, while looking for the weapons.

I was with Hawk, Swole, and Trainer as we dug into the earth. There wasn't much talking going on between us. For my part, it was because I was putting all my effort into the work. We'd already gone down about three feet when Ryder came over from the hole his group had dug.

"Well, we don't have shit over there," he said.

"You found the source of the steel?" Hawk asked. Standing straight, he leaned against the handle of his shovel with the tip buried in the ground.

"Yeah. It's a hunk of metal, looks like it might have been part of some kind of appliance at some point, like a stove or washing machine. God knows how it got into the ground here, but it's useless."

"Fuck," Swole cursed under her breath. "This whole thing is turning into one big pain in the ass."

"Here," Chalupa said, dragging a cooler over to us. "Have a beer and lighten up."

"Eat me," Swole snapped, but she still took a bottle from him.

The rest of us accepted one as well, tossing the twist-off caps to the side. It was a relief to feel the cold liquid slide down my parched throat. Fuck going to the gym. *This* was exercise.

"Holy shit!" We heard Pin's shout from the other side of the property, near where we had parked our bikes.

Happy to have a reason to take a break from digging, I tossed down my shovel along with everyone else and headed in the direction of Pin's group. All four of them were standing around the edge of the pit they had dug, looking down into it.

Did they find the weapons?

"What's up?" I asked.

Pin and Yoda parted to let me see what they were staring at. My eyes widened.

"Is that..."

"Yep," Ryder said, coming up beside me. "That's a dead body."

It wasn't completely uncovered, which I was thankful for, but there was no mistaking the human leg and foot bones that had been uncovered.

"This is where the steel was?" I asked.

Pin picked up a metal detector and held it over the bones. It beeped, and he stared at the readout on the screen.

"Yep."

"It must be a steel medical pin in one of the bones," Hawk said.

"That means the weapons have to be back there," I said, nodding my head in the direction of the hole I'd started with Trainer and the others.

"Agreed," Ryder said. "Cover this up, it doesn't involve us."

Pin and Yoda got to work filling in the hole while the rest of us went back to finally find these damn weapons. I, for one, would be happy to find and get rid of them.

The work went much faster now that there were more of us concentrating in one area. It didn't take long before Trainer's shovel hit a solid object with a dull thunk. We scooped the dirt off the top of what turned out to be a wooden crate.

We uncovered the whole thing, making room on the sides so that four men could get into the hole and lift the heavy crate out. The hole that remained was almost six feet deep.

Ryder ran to his truck and grabbed a crowbar out of the back. We were just losing sunlight when he managed to pry the crate open. There was a white cloth on top, but when Hawk pulled it back, there they were. The crate was packed full of guns. My eyes took in automatic weapons, handguns, and even something big that looked like a sniper rifle.

That was just the stuff I could see. It was high-grade weaponry, just as I'd been told.

Suddenly, a prickling awareness made the fine hairs on the back of my neck stand up. I wasn't sure if it was just a paranoid reaction because I was looking at something so valuable or if someone was really watching us.

"Let's get this thing in the back of my truck," Ryder said. "We'll take it straight to the warehouse."

The warehouse was the place where we stored things like our own weapons or other valuable property. I went to one side of the crate, helping Trainer, Pin, and Swole carry it. The damn thing weighed a ton, but we were almost there. Then, disaster struck.

A tall man with a shaved head and braided mustache stepped out from the far side of Ryder's truck, his black leather jacket blending in with the shadows now that night had fallen. The four us with the crate froze in place while Ryder moved forward, standing between us and the man. Chalupa moved to his side, and the stranger smiled coldly.

"What are you doing here, Mad Dog?"

Fuck.

It was the current leader of Las Balas. I didn't know him because the club had a bad track record with its presidents. They didn't last long. But I'd heard the Mad Dog was a particularly ruthless leader.

"I'm just curious about what you're up to, Ryder. You and your little club here have been snooping around here for a while now. Looks to me like you found something interesting."

"You've been spying on us?" Ryder scoffed. "How

pathetic. Don't you have your own business to worry about?"

"You know, I think that's been the problem with my predecessors. They've ignored the Outlaw Souls for too long. You all are a pain in my ass, and it's time we did something about it."

"We?"

As one, over a dozen men stepped out of the trees lining the property. The bright moonlight glinted off the weapons in their hands, including bats, knives, and even a couple of guns. I scanned the faces for Kat's brother but didn't see him. That made sense, he was just a prospect after all. But I was willing to bet that her dad was among the vicious-looking men.

"Shit," Swole muttered. We were outnumbered and taken by surprise.

"We'll be taking that box," Mad Dog said.

"Like hell, you will," Ryder growled.

Without warning, Mad Dog whipped out a revolver and fired off one shot.

The crate fell to the ground with a crash as the four of us let it go and rushed forward. Ryder crumpled to the ground before any of us reached him. My heart felt like it stopped in my chest, then fired back up at break-neck speed.

Everything happened so fast after that, with the Las Balas men coming at us. Mad Dog stepped back and laughed like a maniac. I didn't usually carry a gun, and I'd never regretted it more. Trainer pulled a gun from under his jacket, while Pin and Yoda hurried to Ryder's side. They grabbed him under the arms, pulling him back behind his truck and as far out of the way as possible with no time to spare. As he went past, I saw that there was blood spreading across his shirt over his lower abdomen.

Fuck. I scanned my surroundings, trying to find something I could use as a weapon.

"Blade," I turned to Kim, who was carrying our shovels, and she threw one to me. I caught it with one hand and used it to block the blow of a man swinging a tire iron at my head.

Swole reappeared with Ryder's crowbar and hit the man on the back of the head hard enough to drop him. I heard two gunshots nearby and felt my heart plummet. This situation had escalated way too quickly, and we weren't prepared. Not only that, but our president was bleeding out somewhere.

Yoda's voice rang out over the struggle going on all around us, "Retreat. I have Ryder."

I looked over to see Yoda was getting into the driver's seat of Ryder's truck. I didn't need to be told twice. Punching the Las Balas man closest to me in the face, I sent him reeling backward and took off toward where we'd parked our bikes. Pin and Kim were at my side, and I could hear others behind us. I just hoped that they were my fellow Outlaw Souls. We needed to get the hell out of here.

I vaguely noticed that the crate was being whisked away by six Las Balas members, but there was nothing we could do about that now.

Ryder's truck fired up and went rocketing forward. Yoda clearly didn't care if he hit any of the fuckers that attacked us. I reached my bike and mounted it, looking up just in time to see that Swole was running toward us, being chased by a big bastard with a baseball bat. I didn't even think as I put my bike into gear and headed straight for them. Passing Swole, I leaned to the right just enough to intercept the man behind her. I wasn't going that fast, so I was able to kick my leg out at the man, catching him in the chest and knocking him flat on his ass. He'd feel that tomorrow.

But the action threw me off-balance, and my bike went in the other direction, too much to keep it upright. It landed on its side, and I felt my ribs—which were already sore from the fight club a couple of days ago—crack. I had no choice but to push through the pain that exploded in my body. I wasn't safe here, not by a long shot.

Picking my bike back up, I saw that the side mirror had broken off, but I didn't need it right now, anyway. I got back on and took off toward the road, joining my brother and sisters as we trailed behind Ryder's truck. We all knew that his injury was serious, and I was sure that they were just as worried as I was. Ryder was a good man and a hell of a leader. I couldn't imagine Outlaw Souls without him.

We all went to the hospital, parking our bikes in the lot as Yoda drove the truck right up to the Emergency Room entrance, running inside for help. I watched as a team of medical staff came hurtling out to the truck, where Ryder was sprawled out in the bed. Every face around me was grim, their anger and fear as potent as my own.

What just happened was a nightmare.

Las Balas had always been our enemy, but this took things to a whole new level. They'd stolen from us and tried to kill our leader. They would pay.

TWO DAYS LATER, I was back at Luca's fighting ring. This time Trainer was with me, and we had an agenda.

It had been a shitty couple of days, with Ryder teetering on the brink of death after major abdominal surgery and the club in disarray over our attack. We had all spent hours in the hospital waiting room that night, ignoring the stares from the staff and family members. I was sure that we looked out of place, and none of us were talking, so that probably didn't help the impression we were giving people.

I felt like I was in shock all night, not sure how to wrap my head around what had happened. It was too surreal. Even the pain of my broken ribs didn't make it feel real.

There was a moment when Swole, Pin, and Trainer all called their wives to tell them what was going on, and I wished I had someone to check in with. I didn't even consider Kat. I knew that she cared about me, no matter how much she tried not to, but she didn't need to know about this. It would just put her in a tough situation.

Maybe she was right about not being together. This was exactly the kind of thing that could come between us, and I didn't think it was ever going to go away. What if I ended up in a physical fight with her brother next time? What if the man I kicked in the chest was her father? She'd never forgive me in either situation.

So, I stayed in my seat in the waiting room, staring at the floor until the doctor came out and told Ryder's wife that he was stable.

Now, we had a plan in place to seek retribution and get the weapons back. We just needed some extra manpower.

"Well, well, well," Luca's voice came from behind me. I turned to see that he had that damn snake draped over his shoulders again. "Look what the cat dragged in."

"Hey, Luca. This is Trainer. Can we talk to you?"

I wanted to get straight to business. We needed to move against Las Balas now, before that sold the weapons they stole from us.

Luca narrowed his eyes at me for a moment, and I waited. I knew him well enough by now to know that he would take his sweet time before making any kind of decision, even something as simple as this.

"All right," he finally said. "Follow me."

This time he led me just outside of the hearing range of the crowd. He clearly had no idea how important this conversation was going to be.

"What's this about?" he asked.

"I know where your weapons are," I said. Luca's gaze flickered to Trainer for a moment before he focused back on me.

"Is that so?"

"Yes. You ever heard of Las Balas?"

Luca's attention on me was laser-sharp as I told him our plan and the part he needed to play in it. By the time we left the warehouse fifteen minutes later, Trainer and I were ready to join the others. We'd be moving against Las Balas tonight.

We pulled into the parking lot of the Blue Dog, where every other member of the club was waiting. I stayed on my bike while Trainer hopped off and addressed the group. He'd stepped up as a leader for us while Ryder was in the hospital, focusing on recovering.

While Trainer gave everyone a rundown on the plan for the evening, Lily, Ryder's sister, walked around the parking lot, giving everyone a braided leather bracelet with a red thread added. She'd made them for each of us to wear tonight in honor of Ryder. The red represented the blood of our brother that was spilled and the reason that we were seeking retribution.

Mad Dog wouldn't survive the night.

We rode out together, the rumble of our motorcycles was a deafening roar that felt powerful. We needed that—to feel like a strong, united group.

The Pit was a rundown bar on the south side of town, and the official hangout of Las Balas. It was where they could be found at all times, and tonight was no different. They must have heard us coming because they were all lined up outside the building when we turned onto the street. They were armed again, but none of the weapons came from the crate.

Good.

We had gambled on their greed making them decide not to use the weapons since they could be sold for so much money. Now we just had to find out where they were. We all parked and dismounted. Tonight, I had a knife on me, but I was supposed to be focused on getting into the bar and trying to find the crate.

It might not be here, but we had to check. Luca's cooperation was dependent on getting those weapons back.

Trainer stood in front of us to address Mad Dog. This was ballsy, seeing as how Ryder was shot last time, but he insisted on doing it. We hoped that they felt secure on their home turf and wouldn't feel the need to try an ambush again. We stayed on the other side of the parking lot for now, and tension hung heavy in the air between the two groups.

I scanned the Las Balas members, and this time, I caught sight of Jason. He looked nervous, and I felt an echo of that within my own body. I thought about Kat again. If something happened to him, I knew she'd be devastated.

"Impressive form," Mad Dog said, addressing Trainer. "Riding in as a unit like that. Much more impressive than the last time we saw you all. Running away with your tail between your legs."

Many of the bikers around him laughed, and I felt a hatred burn within me.

"You know why we're here," Trainer said.

It wasn't a question, but Mad Dog answered anyway.

"I suppose you have a bone to pick with me," He walked back and forth as he talked, looking unconcerned, even though he didn't come closer. "Are you the new fearless leader now? I hear your boy survived, but now's a good time to take control from him. I'd actually admire that."

I couldn't believe that this psycho was having a conversation with Trainer right now. We were here to fight, and everyone knew it.

"We remain loyal to Ryder," Trainer's voice was firm. "The question is, who will replace you?"

Mad Dog opened his mouth to reply, but before another word could be uttered, a shot rang out, cutting through the still night. Moves, our enforcer, did his job, firing just once and sending the bullet straight into Mad Dog's temple.

He was dead before he hit the ground.

Chaos ensued. As expected, the Las Balas members attacked, some shouting out in surprise or anger, while others closed the distance between us without a word. The fight was brutal and wild, with years of pent-up anger and resentment between the two groups making things so much worse. I called on my street fighting experience, focusing on my desire to avenge Ryder as I pummeled those who came at me, careful to avoid their weapons. I could hear the occasional shot going off, but none were near me. I just hoped that no one else I cared about was hit.

"Come on, Blade," Pin called out from my left. He and Hawk were already together. Three of us were supposed to go into the bar to see if the weapons were stashed there. I fought my way through the crowd, stopping only once to pull a man off of Chalupa, who had been knocked to the ground. I made quick work of knocking the guy unconscious with three jabs to the temple before continuing on.

Once we worked our way through the battle, it was easy to get inside the bar. No one was guarding it. They were all in the fight. Just before we went inside, Luca's SUV rolled into the parking lot. His bodyguards got out first, followed by him. Backup had arrived.

Hawk pushed open the door of the bar, leading the way with his gun raised in the air, but no one came running out at us. In fact, there were only two people inside. One of them was a man behind the bar, looking scared, and he ran out the door as soon as he saw us. The other was Jason, and he was hurt.

"Don't," I cried out as Hawk pointed his gun at Jason, who was sitting hunched over at a table with his hand pressed against his bleeding shoulder, right next to his collarbone.

I didn't think Hawk would shoot an injured man, but I couldn't take the chance. I hurried forward and knelt next to him. He didn't seem to recognize me at first, and fear was clear in his eyes, but after a moment, I could see him putting the pieces together.

"Blade?" he asked, his voice weak.

"What happened to you?" I asked, gesturing at his shoulder. I could feel Hawk's eyes on me, but I couldn't explain who Jason was right now.

"Shot, not sure by who," he said, his breathing heavy. "Hurts like a son of a bitch."

"I'll bet it does," I agreed. I looked over at Hawk. Pin had disappeared somewhere. I assumed to check the back room or basement. "I need to get him out of here."

"What? No way. Forget him. We need to find the weapons or get back out there into the fight."

"I can't. He's..." I almost said family, which wasn't true at all. But he was Kat's family, and damn it, I cared about her even if she refused to feel the same. I sighed. "He's important. I need to keep him safe."

Pin came back into the room. "Nothing here that I could find. There are no weapons."

"Damn it, I knew that might happen, but it puts a kink in our plan," Hawk rammed his fist into the wall angrily.

"Let's get back outside," Pin suggested. "We'll subdue a member and make them talk when the fighting is done."

"I'm leaving with Jason," I cut in stubbornly.

"Who the fuck is this guy?" Pin asked, eying Jason suspiciously.

"A prospect," I explained, "and a friend."

Jason looked at me curiously but didn't contradict that last part.

"We need to get out there. And find the weapons."

"I'm sorry," I said. I just couldn't let Jason stay in here bleeding. I knew that Outlaw Souls would be fine. With Luca's help, we outnumbered Las Balas. They didn't need me. Jason did.

Hawk and Pin didn't say anything. They just left me in the bar.

"I'm going to get you out of here," I told Jason.

"Why?"

"For Kat. She's just getting over losing her mom. I won't let her lose you, too."

Surprise flickered through the pain clouding his eyes. "She told you about our mom?"

"Yes, now come on."

I took hold of his good arm and pulled until he was on his feet. Then, I pulled Jason's arm over my shoulder and helped him walk out of there. I was taking him home.

TWENTY-FIVE
KAT

I hadn't seen Blade in days. I knew that it shouldn't bother me, given the nature of our relationship, but I couldn't help frowning as I looked over at his empty workstation. He'd called Brie this morning to tell her that he wouldn't be in today and to reschedule his appointments. She said he didn't elaborate on why he was taking the day off, and she assumed that he was sick.

I had a feeling that something else was going on.

I had tried to get a hold of him yesterday, Sunday afternoon, to see if I could come over for a booty call, but his only reply to my text was to say that he was unavailable. It was stupid to feel rejected—the guy had a life outside of our casual sex—but I didn't like it one bit. I worried that he was getting bored with our arrangement.

Then, I chastised myself for such an insecure overreaction. One polite decline didn't mean anything. But now, seeing that he wasn't at work, I couldn't shake the feeling of foreboding that hung over me. Somehow, I knew that something was wrong.

I had just finished up with a client, an eighteen-year-old

girl that wanted a butterfly on her ankle, and Piper was waiting for a customer that she'd been working with for the last few days to come in so that she could put the finishing touches on his full sleeve. I was chomping away on my gum, wishing that I had a damn cigarette on me.

"So, you're tense," Piper remarked, sipping from her Styrofoam cup of coffee. Piper was a caffeine junkie, so she usually had one in the morning *and* brought one back from lunch with her. I liked to tease her about it, but I didn't have much room to talk since I guzzled sweet energy drinks to keep myself going. "Where's Blade today?"

"How should I know?" I shrugged.

"Cut that shit out," she said impatiently. "It's *me,* Kat. I know you."

"I still don't know where he is."

"So, *that's* what's bothering you. Have you called him?"

"I'm not his wife," I said. "Not even his girlfriend. He doesn't owe me an explanation."

"No, he doesn't. But I bet he'd give you one."

I picked up on something in her slightly clipped tone. Disapproval?

"You have a problem with Blade now?"

"Of course not. But I think that it's about time you decided what you want."

"I have what I want. Great sex, no commitment, and plenty of freedom."

"He had that freedom too, you know. He could go out and find someone that's not too hung up on daddy's approval to see that she's blowing it with a guy that might be her perfect match."

"Ouch," I grimaced.

"The truth hurts," Piper said unapologetically.

"And I'm not trying to get my dad's approval. I just..." I trailed off.

Why *was* I so loyal to Las Balas? Because Mad Dog had called me family? It was a nice sentiment, but it would have been even nicer to be treated like family by my dad. The problem was that Las Balas came first, always. Maybe I thought that aligning myself with them would put me in that category for my dad.

That was pathetic. And to think that I had been silently judging Jason for letting Las Balas control his life. I was doing that same thing without even having the option to join the club. They were old fashioned in their no-girls-allowed stance. In reality, I had almost nothing to do with the club, and the more time I spent with Blade, the more skeptical I was of Outlaw Souls being troublemakers. Still, I'd taken a stand, and it wasn't easy to backtrack at this point.

"You can do whatever you want," Piper said, "but I think you need to realize that you can only keep Blade at arm's length for so long before you lose your grip on him altogether. Because I can tell you right now, he has real feelings for you."

I wanted to argue, but the words wouldn't come.

The bell above the door rang, and Piper stood. Her customer was here.

"Take my advice or don't. It's up to you. I just don't want to see you lonely anymore."

She knew me too well. For the rest of the day, I couldn't get her words out of my mind. When I first found out that Blade was an Outlaw Soul, I had been sure that he must be a bad person to be a part of an organization like that. But as I continued to get to know him, I knew that I was wrong. He was a good man.

But I couldn't let my guard down with him again. I couldn't let myself trust him.

Look where that's gotten you.

We were stuck in a limbo where we fucked and fought over and over. It was exhausting, and mostly my fault. I knew that. Looking back over the last few weeks, I could see that I picked fights with Blade every time I started to feel too close to him, as if I was proving to him and myself that we were incompatible.

God, I was an idiot.

I wanted to be with Blade. Hell, I'd wanted him from the moment we met. When he got his patch, we'd only been together once, and I told myself that I wasn't attached to him yet. There hadn't been enough time.

But I was wrong. I was starting to suspect that I'd fallen for him the first time he sent a flirty smirk in my direction.

My heart rate tripled, and I felt like a curtain had been pulled back in my mind, revealing what had been hidden just out of sight for so long. I wanted to be with Blade. I wanted it more than I wanted to connect with my dad. Because now that Piper had suggested it, I realized that was exactly what I was doing. I was trying to chase an elusive relationship with my dad through the damn motorcycle club that always meant more to him than I did. It was never going to happen, but I could have something good with Blade if I hadn't blown it already.

I could hardly wait to get through the rest of the day after this revelation. I sent a text to Blade, simply asking if he was available to meet up this evening, but after almost an hour with no response, I felt my heart sink.

Why didn't he respond? What was he up to?

THAT EVENING, I went to Piper's house for our weekly poker game. I was distracted by my annoyingly silent cell phone, which made me a better player, to my surprise. I wasn't too focused on the cards, making me a hell of a bluffer, and I wasn't overthinking everything.

I still hadn't heard back from Blade.

"You won't believe what I heard," Veronica was saying as she shuffled the cards. I was only half-listened to the conversation at this point. Tammy had been prattling on and on about her wedding plans for the last twenty minutes. I loved the woman, but it wasn't the most interesting topic. Besides, I wasn't in a good headspace to discuss her happily ever after.

"Oh, are we gossiping?" Piper asked as she walked in with a fresh beer for me and a glass of wine for herself.

"Most definitely," Veronica winked. I took the beer from Piper's outstretched hand and was in the middle of my first sip when Veronica continued, "Last night, someone shot the president of that motorcycle club. I think they're called the Outlaws."

I nearly choked.

"Outlaw Souls," Piper corrected, shooting me a concerned look.

I gulped, swallowing the beer in my mouth so that I could speak.

"How do you know this?" I asked, the panic in my voice was clear, but I didn't care. Blade calling into work the day after Ryder takes a bullet was too much of a coincidence. What if he was hurt too?

I really hoped this had nothing to do with Las Balas, but I wasn't naive. They were enemies, after all.

"I'm good friends with one of the ER nurses over at La Playa Regional Hospital. She said he was brought in two nights ago with a bullet in his gut. Had to have surgery to get it out."

I needed to see Blade. I had to make sure that he was okay. I could tell that he cared about Ryder when he came in for a tattoo. This must be killing him. I also wanted to make sure that he knew I had his back, no matter what. I wasn't a member of Las Balas, no matter how much I had been acting like it. I was his girl all along, even if I didn't realize it.

"I need to go," I said, putting my cards down and standing.

"Is something wrong?" Tammy asked. Veronica looked concerned, too, but Piper just gave me a small smile.

"I have to go see Blade," I told Piper. She'd explain the situation to the others. I didn't want to waste time.

I wasn't sure where Blade would be tonight, but I decided to try his apartment first. If he wasn't there, I'd go to the Outlaw Souls bar, the Blue Dog. I'd never been there before, but I knew where it was.

I left Piper's house and had just gotten into my car when my cell phone rang. I answered it immediately without even pausing to check the caller ID, hoping it would be Blade.

"Hello?"

"Kat."

"Lexie?"

It was Jason's girlfriend, and I could tell that she was crying. It was as though a fist had just reached into my chest and started squeezing my heart. There must be something wrong with Jason.

"What's happened?" I asked sharply, needing her to talk to me. I started up the car and headed in the direction of Jason's apartment building.

"It's Jason. He's been hurt."

"Is he in the hospital?"

There was no way this was a coincidence. Ryder was shot, and now Jason was injured. What the hell was going on between Las Balas and Outlaw Souls?

"No, he's home with me. He said no to going to the hospital. They'd ask too many questions. It's just that he looks so pale, and there's so much blood."

I beat down my own frantic reaction to her words. Lexie was pregnant and clearly terrified. She needed me to be as calm as possible to help her through this.

"I'm five minutes away," I told her as I broke pretty much every speeding law that La Playa had. "Is he awake?"

"Yes. He wants to see you."

"What kind of wound does he have?"

"He says he..." her breath hitched, and I suspected that she was suppressing a sob. "He says he was shot."

"Fuck."

"I can't do this anymore, Kat," she said. "I can't deal with this Las Bala shit anymore."

Uh-oh.

I pulled up in front of their apartment building. "I'm here. Buzz me in."

I hung up the phone as she did. Their apartment was on the second floor, so I hit the stairs, not wanting to wait for the elevator.

When I knocked on the apartment door, it was pulled open immediately.

"Kat," Lexie threw her thin body into mine, giving me a fierce hug. I patted her back and made soothing noises.

"Where is he?"

"Our bedroom," she sniffled.

Disengaging from Lexie, I stepped inside and headed to

the hallway off the kitchen, where there were two bedrooms. I saw bloody rags in the sink and forced myself to look away.

"Jason?" I called out as I knocked on the cracked door.

"Come in," he said.

I found him lying on top of the blankets, shirtless. I could see streaks of dark red where blood had been wiped away. There was a clean bandage on his shoulder, with just a hint of red in the center, where blood was starting to bleed through.

"What the fuck happened?" I asked, trying not to sound like I was accusing him of anything.

"It's a long story," he sighed and gestured to the empty spot on the bed next to him. I sat down.

"I've got time."

He sighed. "I think that the first thing you should know is that Blade probably saved my life tonight."

"Blade," I echoed, trying to make sure I heard him correctly.

"Yeah. There was a big fight tonight between Las Balas and Outlaw Souls. Actually, it technically started a couple of days ago."

"When Ryder was shot?"

"How did you know that?"

"A friend of a friend," I said vaguely. "It doesn't matter. Just tell me what happened."

He did, beginning with Las Balas taking the crate of weapons that the Outlaw Souls dug up. Jason wasn't there, but he knew what happened. The entire club was abuzz with the news that Mad Dog had tried to kill Ryder. Then, he filled me in on everything that happened tonight, the way that Blade had stood up to his Outlaw Souls brothers and gotten Jason out of there.

I beat back tears that threatened to fill my eyes. Blade had done this for me. I was sure of it. He saved my brother because Jason was so important to me. I couldn't stand to lose him after my mother's passing, and Blade knew that. After losing his own brother, he probably understood it more than most.

"He brought me here and patched up my shoulder. Luckily, the bullet went all the way through. So, he stitched me up, and we had a little chat."

"About?"

Please don't say you talked about me.

"The missing crate of weapons that we stole."

Right, of course. I felt stupid for thinking they'd be discussing me. There were clearly more important things to deal with.

"You know where they are?" I asked.

"Yep, and now Blade does, too."

"I can't believe you betrayed Las Balas."

"I'm done with them. This whole thing was about greed and hatred, and I'm done with that. People died, and I could've been one of them. What if I'd bled out while they were fighting? I would have left Lexie and our kid behind, and for what? Some money that the club would keep? Besides, there's a lot you don't know about Las Balas, none of it good."

"So, tell me," I said, eager to finally hear the truth. "I need to know."

Jason sighed and leaned his head back on his pillow with his eyes closed, but after a moment, he started to speak.

"Well, they have a history in some pretty notorious shit. Human trafficking, for instance. They kidnapped young girls and sold them."

My stomach rolled. My god, I had no idea they'd *ever* done something like that. It was horrifying.

"When did they do that?"

"It went on for a long time," he said. "They really just stopped a few years ago, mostly because Outlaw Souls got involved in shutting that shit down."

"So, Dad..."

He nodded solemnly. "Dad was involved in it."

I felt like my entire world shifted beneath my feet. I had always known that my dad was a selfish ass that devoted his life to Las Balas, but I *never* thought he'd do something like that. Those poor girls...

Blade must think I'm a complete idiot for giving these people my loyalty.

"There's also heavy drug use and distributing, stealing, arms dealing. The list goes on. Basically, any illegal activity that could make them money, no matter how immoral it is."

I remembered something from our conversation a few days ago. "You told me that Outlaw Souls harassed Rage's girlfriend last year. Was that a lie?"

"Not really, but Rage had built a fucking meth lab in her basement, so some could argue that they had a good reason to bust up in there and clear that shit out."

I shook my head in disgust. Nothing was quite what I thought it was.

"Why have you been trying to join for so long if you knew all this?"

"I don't know anymore." He scrubbed a hand down his face tiredly. "At first, it was to see what the big deal was. Why dad and others were so into it. And I'll admit, there is something appealing about the comradery. Then, I had this relationship with Dad, and I don't know...I guess that I convinced myself it wasn't that bad. I know it sounds stupid."

It did, but it was also so stupid of me to reject Blade when Las Balas was clearly the problem in La Playa. I had to make that right if he'd let me.

"You need to tell Lexie that you're walking away," I advised him. "Because she's at the end of her rope right now."

"I know." Guilt was clear in the lines of his face. "I've been so stupid when it comes to her. It's a miracle she puts up with me."

"That's what you do when you love someone," I said, standing. "So, are you okay? Do you need anything?"

"No, I'm good. Are you going to talk to Blade?"

I nodded.

"Good. He's a good guy, I think."

"I think so, too," I smiled.

"Send my girl in on your way out, okay? I want to tell her the good news."

"I'll call you tomorrow," I told him before leaving the room.

I didn't have to tell Lexie to go see him. She was already heading that way with a tray of food. He was so lucky to have someone that cared enough to take care of him. There was a pang in the center of my chest at that thought. Did I have that?

There was only one way to find out.

It was late when I left Jason's apartment, and I was tempted to text or call Blade, but what I needed to say to him had to be said in person. So, I went home, deciding that I would talk to him tomorrow, no matter what.

TWENTY-SIX
BLADE

"So, you found the weapons?" Ryder asked around a mouthful of food as he sat up in the hospital bed. I had brought him a fast-food breakfast sandwich since he'd been complaining about the hospital food for the past few days.

"Yeah, the entire crate was in the basement of Mad Dog's house. Apparently, he didn't trust anyone else with it. He'd already talked to a couple of people about buying, but it doesn't seem like he'd lined up a buyer yet."

"Good," Ryder said, polishing off the sandwich and popping a hash brown into his mouth. "Now, tell me about this prospect you got the info from."

I felt a surprising protectiveness swell within me. I didn't want Jason dragged into this any more than he had been. Yes, he made a shitty choice by trying to join Las Balas, but he didn't know any better. Kat was a prime example of that.

"He's my girl's brother," I said, hoping that Ryder would understand that he was off-limits without me having to say it. I didn't want to be at odds with anyone in the club. "And he's decided to leave Las Balas."

"I see," Ryder looked thoughtful. "You know, my sister's boyfriend was once a Las Balas prospect. Sometimes, it just takes time for people to realize how poisonous they are."

There was a knock on the door, and Chalupa walked in. "Luca followed through. We gave him the weapons, and he's already packing up his operations in La Playa. He'll be gone by tonight."

"Thank fuck for that," Ryder said, and I shared the sentiment.

"Moves's going to keep an eye on the situation and let us know if Luca goes back on his word, but somehow, I don't think he will."

"Me either," I chimed in. "When I talked to him at the warehouse, he seemed pretty eager to get back home to El Paso."

"What about our people?" Ryder asked. "Injuries? Deaths?"

"One death," Chalupa said, his face dropping. "Tank took a bullet to the chest."

Tank was fiercely loyal and took a bullet for his brothers in the MC. He was fearless. "He bled out at the scene, but we brought him home so that we could take care of him."

"God damn it," Ryder sighed, and I saw his hand go to his stomach where he'd been shot. Not only had we lost a good man and brother, but it made us all a little more aware of our mortality.

"Other than that, it was mostly superficial cuts and bruises. Swole had a broken finger, and Hawk got sliced in the side with a knife, needing stitches. They'll both be fine."

"Well, that's something to be thankful for," Ryder said. "Now, we'll just have to stay vigilant. Things are heating up with Las Balas, and I'm sure it's not over yet. From what I understand, we took out four of their people last night, including Mad Dog. I didn't want it to come to that, but sometimes it's kill or be killed, and I always have a scar to remind me of that."

"We'll all do what we have to do to protect our own," Chalupa agreed.

We left after that. Ryder's wife was coming in to visit him, and he wanted some time alone with her. Besides, I needed some sleep. I had been awake almost all night. First, I patched up Jason, then I went to Mad Dog's house and found the crate. I took charge of the hand-off with Luca, making sure that he got exactly what he came here for. Finally, I met with the rest of the club at the Blue Dog, where I learned of Tank's fate and reported that I had found the weapons.

Now, it was almost seven in the morning. The sun was already too bright in the sky, and the people I passed on my bike were heading to work, just beginning their day. I felt like a zombie by comparison.

I went into my apartment and made a beeline for the bedroom. I could barely think due to exhaustion, but I managed to call Brie and tell her I needed one more day off. She was fine with it, and for the first time, I truly appreciated what a good boss she was.

That was the last conscious thought I remembered having before I laid out on my bed, fully clothed, and fell asleep.

I WAS VIOLENTLY YANKED from a peaceful sleep by an incessant pounding on the front door of my apartment. It was disorienting to come back into the world of consciousness so quickly, and I sat up in bed, confused about where the annoying noise was coming from. A quick glance at the alarm clock's big red numbers told me that I had been asleep for about twelve hours.

Someone knocked again, and I finally realized what was going on. Who the hell was bugging me now?

"Hold your horses," I called out, pulling back my sheets and getting out of the bed. My body was aching from sleeping for so long, and my head felt heavy. As I reached the door, I opened it without bothering to check the peephole while in the middle of a massive yawn.

Kat was standing on the other side, looking like a sex goddess in her black fishnet top with a completely visible black bra underneath and a pair of black leather pants. My cock stood at attention so quickly that I thought it might actually pop the zipper of my jeans.

But I didn't let myself get too excited at the sight of her. By now, I was sure that Jason had told her all about what happened last night. If she was here to give me shit about Outlaw Souls *attacking* Las Balas, I wasn't in the mood to listen to it.

I must have been standing there for too long without speaking because she shifted her weight from one foot to the other and bit her lip nervously.

"You weren't at work," she said.

"No, I wasn't."

I stepped away from the door, leaving it open for her if she decided to come in, and went to my kitchen, grabbing a bottle of water. I was parched, so I drank half the thing in one go. When I turned around, Kat was standing behind me.

"Are you okay?"

What a loaded question. I was happy that Outlaw Souls had won this battle but upset at the loss of Tank. More than anything else, though, I was sick of this back and forth between the two of us. Kat was an addiction that I didn't mind one bit, but if she really didn't want me, I wasn't interested in sleeping together anymore. Who knew that I'd grow sick of this casual sex thing?

"No, I don't think I am."

"Can I do anything for you?" she asked, stepping closer as she looked up at me through her eyelashes.

"Tell me why you're here."

"I know what happened last night."

I sighed, "I'm not in the mood for a fight about Outlaw Souls."

I'd just slept for twelve hours, but this conversation was still tiring.

"No," she stepped even closer, and the sweet scent of her wrapped around me. God, my body always burned for her. "I want to thank you for getting Jason out of there. His shitty club members probably wouldn't have done it."

"He's your brother. I know how precious that is."

"He told me the truth about Las Balas, all the terrible shit they've done. I really had no idea. I feel like a complete jackass."

I cupped her chin, running my thumb across her smooth cheek.

"Don't be so hard on yourself," I said. "You've been, like, half a jackass, at most."

I chuckled as she slapped my arm, but there was a smile in her eyes.

"Come on, it's not easy to admit I'm wrong."

I was just so damn relieved that she was finally coming around that I didn't need her to admit anything, except that she was mine.

"Okay, fine. You've come to your senses. Glad to hear

it," my eyes flickered down to her lips. "Now, what are you going to do about it?"

I barely had time to brace myself before Kat literally jumped into my arms. She hugged my neck while her legs went around my waist. Her lips pressed against mine, and it was all blazing fire and needy passion. This woman was always my undoing, bringing out the animal in me. Right now, that animal needed to claim what was his.

I started to walk us into my bedroom, not even breaking our kiss, as I was familiar with the layout of my own place. Just before we reached my bedroom, a tantalizing thought occurred to me, and I shifted directions, taking her into the bathroom.

"What are we doing?" she asked, pulling her head back to look around.

"I need to take a shower. You want to join me?"

"Please."

I set Kat down on her feet, and she stripped out of her clothes while I turned on the shower, so that when I turned around, all I could see was creamy skin. Her nipples were hard little buds in the cool air, begging for me to taste.

I started to unbutton my jeans, and she stepped into the shower, letting out a husky moan that made my erection throb. I nearly tripped trying to get out of my jeans and boxers so that I could join her.

The warm water ran over her body in rivulets, and I found myself transfixed by it until she reached out and took hold of my cock. I had to catch myself on the tiled wall as she started to pump her hand up and down. Pleasure licked up my spine from something so simple, but when she got on her knees in front of me, a deep-rooted excitement took hold.

But I didn't want her to do this just to make things up to

me, "You don't have to do that," I told her, reaching down to pull her up by her arms.

"I want to," she insisted, flicking her tongue out and running it over the tip of my cock. It felt like I was hit with an electric jolt.

"Shit," I hissed, staring down at her. The wicked smile she shot me might have been the sexiest thing I'd ever seen until she opened her plump lips and swallowed my cock.

I moaned loud and long as the sensations caused by her mouth spread all over my body. She took me all the way in until I butted up against the back of her throat. Then, she moaned, and the vibrations from that action brought me so close to an orgasm that I felt like an inexperienced teenager again.

Fuck, she was good at this.

I beat back the orgasm with sheer force of will. I wanted this to last longer. I *needed* it.

Wrapping her hand around the base of my cock, Kat pumped my shaft as she worked her mouth up and down. She got into a rhythm that drove me crazy. It felt so good but was just languorous enough to keep me on the edge of nirvana.

The water beat down on my back, seeming to heighten the sensation by making my skin feel more sensitive, and when Kat reached around with her free hand and grabbed a handful of my ass, pulling me forward and deep-throating my cock, I lost it. My orgasm slammed into me with no time to warn her before I exploded into her wet, warm mouth. But it didn't matter to her. She swallowed every drop of what I gave her, looking up into my eyes in one of the most intimate moments we'd ever shared.

"I fucking love you," I said without stopping to think about it. I got caught up in the moment. If I'd stopped to consider what I was going to say, I probably would have held the words back. I didn't know where she was emotionally, and putting myself out there like that felt like a good way to scare her away again.

To my surprise, Kat smiled as she got to her feet. Cupping my cheek, she looked into my eyes, and I could see nothing but happiness there.

"I love you, too," she said.

"You do?"

I didn't mean to sound like an insecure child, but I really didn't think she'd say it back.

"I do. I can't believe it took me so long to realize it, but I love you for the things you do. I've always thought that actions were more important than words, and your actions say so much. The way that you pursued me. The way you helped me find a bike. The way you helped my brother. You've shown me who you are, and I couldn't help falling for you, no matter how hard I tried."

"And your stubborn ass put up a hell of a fight," I said, earning me another slap on the arm.

"Watch it, or I might just go home," she said, but I knew it was an empty threat.

There was no way she was leaving now. My cock was already hardening again.

"I'll have you know, I like your stubborn ass," I said, reaching around to pinch her.

She squealed, and I shut off the water. A proper shower could come later. For now, I wanted to get Kat into my bed. If actions were more important to her than words, she was going to love what happened next.

EPILOGUE: KAT

I bent over and peered through the window in front of the oven, checking the roast beef for the hundredth time. I'd never made something like this before, but I really wanted to do something impressive, something worthy of my mom. We were resuming Sunday family meals at my house, so Jason and Lexie would be here in an hour.

The sound of breaking glass came from behind me, followed by Blade's curse, "Shit!"

I popped up and turned to see that he had dropped a wine glass onto the floor, where it shattered into a thousand pieces. He looked at me with the cutest guilty smile on his face. I couldn't help laughing.

"It's okay," I told him. "Lexie can't drink anyway, remember?"

Lexie was the reason we hadn't started doing this sooner. I wanted to start the tradition back up again when Blade moved in with me a month ago, breaking his old lease a few months early, but Lexie was having a hell of a tough time with morning sickness, which it turned out could occur at any time. She even lost almost ten pounds because she couldn't hold down any food, but she was starting to make up for it now. She had a little baby bump that I couldn't wait to see growing into a huge pregnant belly. I had no interest in parenting myself, but I was excited to spoil a niece or nephew in six months.

"Right," he said. "I'll just give her a water glass."

Blade was so supportive when I told him about my old Sunday dinner tradition, insisting on helping me in any way that he could, even though he was mostly helpless in the kitchen. So, I had him set the table.

Looking around, I couldn't believe that this was the same house that had felt so lonely to me just a few months ago. I had redecorated every room, knowing that was what my mom would have wanted. Now it was really my place. No, it was *our* place. Living with Blade made me happy to be home. I liked waking up to his face and falling asleep in his arms every night.

Blade was no longer street fighting. When he told me about it, I was mortified. I knew that there were no rules in the ring at those places, and he could end up seriously hurt or even killed. Luca might have left town, but another one would crop up, eventually. They always did. I didn't tell Blade that he had to stop, but when he saw how worried I was, he promised not to do it anymore. He said that talking to me about his brother helped. I hoped it was true. He'd done so much to help me, I wanted to be there for him, to help him fight his own demons.

I finished up my meal while Blade swept up the broken glass and finished setting the table. The roasted beef was sliced on a platter, and there were bowls of glazed carrots and mashed potatoes on the stove. I'd followed recipes that I had found written on index cards in my mom's handwriting in a small metal box. It was a little nerve-wracking to cook such a nice meal by myself for the first time, but it also brought back some of the best memories that I had of my mom. Just the smells wafting through the house seemed to transport me back in time.

"This looks amazing, Kitten," Blade said, coming up behind me and kissing the side of my neck.

"Thank you," I said as pride ballooned within me.

He reached around and tried to snag a piece of beef, but I slapped his hand away. "No way, mister. This is for everyone."

He pouted playfully. "Haven't you ever heard of quality control? Someone should taste it to make sure it tastes good. I'm willing to take the risk for you."

I turned around, putting my arms around his neck. "You're such a hero."

Blade took my lips in a kiss, but at that moment, the door of the house opened, and Jason called out, "We're here, guys. Coming into the house. Is the coast clear?"

I chuckled as I pulled my mouth away from Blade's and called out. "Yeah, come on in."

Jason used to walk right into my house unannounced all the time, but now he was more cautious since two days after Blade moved in, he'd walked in to find the two of us butt-naked on the couch, in the middle of wild sex.

Now, he claimed to be scarred for life and insisted on announcing his arrival. He still didn't bother to just knock and wait for us to answer the door, though. I guessed it was just a habit from having grown up here.

He and Lexie came in, Lexie holding a pie. I had requested that they take care of dessert because I was already exceeding my own limits by making the meal. Baking was just out of the question.

"Coconut cream pie," Lexie said, popping it into the refrigerator for later.

"Yum," Blade said, and I put a hand on his arm.

"Don't even think about going near that fridge."

"What do you think I am, some kind of animal?"

"Aren't you?"

"Only in the bedroom," he smirked.

"Hey, not on family dinner day," Jason said, his nose scrunched up and a look of disgust on his face. "You've done enough damage to my fragile psyche."

I threw the dish towel at him across the table, and he dodged it like it was a bullet.

"Come on, Jason, help me with the drinks," Blade said.

I watched for a moment as the two most important men in my life worked together to fill up the wine glasses and get Lexie some water. It wasn't really a two-person job, but I appreciated the effort. The two of them had become fast friends after that night at the Pit, which just showed that belonging to rival motorcycle clubs didn't really affect much in the grand scheme of things.

Jason's decision to leave Las Balas was a good one, but it had been poorly received by our father. I hadn't talked to my dad since the night that I drove him home drunk, and I had no plans to reach out to him anymore. Since Jason had filled me in on the gritty details of Las Balas activities, I couldn't look at him the same anymore. In fact, knowing that my father had played a part in human trafficking even though he had a daughter of his own made my stomach turn.

I was finally done with the man, after so many years of hoping to connect on some level, somehow. I pushed thoughts of my dad aside and focused on Lexie, who was leaning against the counter, also watching our men.

"Penny for your thoughts?" I asked.

"I was just thinking that things are so much better since Jason left Las Balas. I feel like I have him back again, you know? It's not just that he has more time for me, either. When he was a prospect, he seemed troubled, even when we *did* spend time together. It was like he was never really away from them."

"Yeah, I'm just glad that they never made him a full patch."

He'd never been directly involved in anything illegal because he wasn't a member of the club, so when he withdrew from Las Balas, they let him go. It might have been more difficult if he was more involved with their activities.

I carried the meat platter to the table while Lexie got the vegetables. When we all sat around the table, I was overcome with emotion. It was like my mom was still here. I looked toward Blade, but he was blurry as tears filled my eyes. I smiled at him.

"You know, Mom would have really liked to meet you," I said. "She was such a great mom, always taking care of me and Jason. And she was so funny."

"Yeah," Jason agreed. "She had some old-school wit that could even slay Kat."

I laughed. "That's true. No one could compare."

We spent the rest of the meal sharing stories about her. I was able to chase away the tears with laughter as Jason talked about the trouble he got into as a teenager, and how our mom always said he made her go grey about ten years early. It felt good to remember her like this, with the people that I loved most around me while we enjoyed food created from her recipes.

This was happiness, and I couldn't believe that I was lucky enough to find it again. Reaching over, I took hold of Blade's hand, interlacing our fingers. As long as I had him to hold onto, I knew that I'd always feel content. He was my biker, and I was his Kitten 'till the end.

WHAT'S NEXT?

Turn the page to find out where it all began for The Outlaw Souls MC and **grab your FREE copy of The Prequel**! I'll also give you a sneak peak into the in the next book in the series, *Diego*!

GET YOUR FREE BOOK!

Hey hey!
*Get your **FREE copy of Outlaw Souls: The Prequel**
sent directly to your inbox. You'll also be the first to hear
about upcoming new releases, giveaways, cover reveals,
chapter reveals, and much more.*

CLICK HERE To Get Your Free Book

DIEGO

You don't want to miss the rest of the **Outlaw Souls series**! If you enjoyed *BLADE* check out my next book of the series called *DIEGO*.

CLICK HERE To Read DIEGO Now!

***DIEGO* Book Blurb:**

A nomad rider who vowed to escape his past. Until it came back to haunt him.

La Playa carried too many painful secrets of his past. He wanted a clean slate. What was a bad boy rider like Diego be doing with Misty, a hot Latina doctor to be?

All he knows is they were like two moths to one another's flame. But an Outlaw gang member can't be caught in a secret love affair, can he?

Diego is a free spirited rider searching for his place in the world.

But... A forbidden love threatens to tear their families apart...

Will their love withstand a gang war or they rise together forged from the fire?

Click here to find out for yourself. Happy reading!

PREVIEW: DIEGO

An MC Romance (Outlaw Souls Book 5)
A Sneak Peak

1. DIEGO

Riding on the wings of freedom. Or as close as a man can come to it. I weaved slowly through the Pacific Highway traffic, the wind breezing past my face and the soft throttle of my Harley Davidson leading me to my next destination. My chopper took me where I needed to be. Right now the road was leading to an unknown destination somewhere along the Californian coast. Just how I liked it. Things had changed drastically since Ryder took over from Padre as President of the Outlaw Souls. The chapter roster was switching up and people were being shuffled around the chessboard. I wanted out. My restless bones wanted someplace fresh and new. Someplace where people didn't know my name. With the changeover, my nomad patch stripes came into full effect and I got my chance.

"It's what Padre would have wanted. The floor is yours." Yoda, Padre's brother and chapter chaplain sealed it at the Blue Dog Saloon meeting before I left. Music to my ears because the town of La Playa was...well, played out.

"You've officially been given your nomad stripes. Padre

always wanted to open a new chapter and expand the operation," Yoda explained.

"Then I'm the man to do it."

"Job's all yours, Diego. I approve of it." Yoda nodded while shaking my hand.

My essentials were neatly packed in my leased apartment. Ready to go. I would sort out the rest from wherever I landed. My heart had been calling me to leave for years. But I met someone that slowed my progress down. A beautiful woman. After things went sour with Crystal, I felt a sense of relief. I still wanted to remain loyal to the chapter, but the desperate ache to spread my wings made me jump at the chance to leave.

My chopper continued gliding smoothly through the California traffic as my stomach rumbled, telling me it was about time to stop and eat. No sad goodbyes and no heavy hearts neither. I wasn't the man for that. When I moved on I liked to cut it clean. I planned on staying within the borders of California. I would know when to put the kickstand down. My plan was to check in somewhere and land where I felt best. That was as far as I got with it.

Thinking back to when I first met, things with Crystal probably deteriorated over time. I used to frequent Marty's every Friday night. One Friday, I rode in solo and parked myself in a good spot. A mixed crowd of both men and women were out for the night, crimson lighting flooding the stage. I'd found myself a nice little spot close by. I was ready to kick back with some entertainment, maybe drop a little change. A tanned blonde with legs for days, ample curves and a pouty mouth graced the stage, making me sit up. Her moves on the stripper pole were more sensual than the other girls, not so grimy. The difference with her was her body looked natural and soft; no enhancements like I saw with the other strippers.

"Who the hell is that?" I'd tapped the shoulder of the bartender Alice, who I was on a first-name basis with. She put my beer in front of me.

"Ah, you like the look of her? That's Crystal, she just started here last week." I inched forward to get a better look. Her eyes met mine and I knew it was on. That was all it took with me. Eye contact. Took a few more visits before anything ramped up between us.

One midnight hour two years ago, that changed as Crystal slid towards me. "You come here all the time. I think it's about time you take me on a date." A long tongue suggestion and a kitten crawl across the stage would get you a date real quick with me.

"Sure. We can work something out." Heavy breasts jiggled as she swayed like fluid water to her feet.

"Sounds good, big boy. Meet you after my set. Drop them fifties right in here." She pointed to the elastic of her g-string. Of course I did. Any man in their right mind would. Just like that, we got started in a relationship that lasted two years. I grew to love her. But it wasn't enough. We got into it one night at my place.

"I don't want to strip anymore. I have enough saved to take a break for a while. Can't we think about taking the next step? I want a family with you." That cutesy voice I liked had become whiny to me, making my skin crawl as soon as she said it.

"It's not what I want. I'm not ready to settle down right now. I respect that's what you want. But honey, it's not for me." The tears flowed, I comforted her as best I could. I knew the man I was inside.

"I didn't mean it. I mean, I can live without them. I just

thought we had something." Crystal stroked my face and I left her with a kiss.

"We did, but it's run its course. If you want kids, I don't want to rob you of that decision." I rubbed her hands. I wanted to have some level of compassion. "You're going to find someone just your vibe. I'm not your guy." Sometimes my honesty got me into trouble. Led to heartbreak. Might be part of the reason my name Diego the "Dog" Christopher fit me as a name. Women never called me that to my face, thankfully. My devilish charm usually won them over. I remained friends with most of the women I banged. Even had a few of them on replay. Just depended on the season and the timing. But I treated all of them with the respect they deserved, which was why they kept coming back. Others in the club might have argued I got my nickname because of my loyalty.

So that was how it was left. No ties. Just the wind puffing up the back of my jacket and a hamburger joint coming up. I'd been riding for three hours and that was about my limit in any given stretch. Time to let my long limbs have a rest. Standing six-feet-two could have its advantages, but on a bike, it could tighten up the legs a little. I kinda wished I took the coastal route. To have some of the ocean spray hit me in the face along the way. But for some reason, I chose to stick to the Pacific Highway. The sign said "Bakersfield" as I pulled up to an old-school diner. I parked and stretched, taking in the clear blue California sky. A few large trucks were parked on the gravel driveway as I pushed through the screen door. The familiar sizzle of hamburgers on the grill and the distinct smell of onions made my mouth water. *Wouldn't mind a beer as well.* However, I was riding so I'd wait. A Mom and Pop hamburger joint, right up my alley. Anytime I rode out and found a good place to stop off for food, I stored it in the memory bank for the next ride. A few truckers were in the booths, making their stops and reading the paper. The sound of the radio flowed through the diner.

"Hey, good looking. On a stop? What can I get ya'?"

I gave the lady behind the counter a big grin. I liked her spunk. A little dumpy probably, in her early fifties with brown hair stuck to her forehead from the Cali heat. She was wearing an old apron. It was just her out front with a rectangular peephole where the meals were being placed behind the counter. An older man with a net was whipping up the meals in the back. I looked up at the chalk menu board.

"Yep. Just passing through. I'm looking at that mega burger. I'll take it. Don't leave anything out," I replied.

"Okay." She laughed and her stomach heaved along with her. "That's a mighty fine bike you got out there." She pointed to it.

"Sure is. My pride and joy."

"I can see why. We get some bikers that roll through here from time to time. Check out those mags in the rack if you want." She pointed to a pile of magazines in the middle of the diner. "Take a seat and I'll bring your burger out. Help yourself to water on the side there."

"Will do." My meal came out ten minutes later. I devoured the juicy hamburger with everything included. I washed it down with juice. I sat out front of the takeaway, flicking through a local bike magazine. I stopped a few pages in. A bunch of old dudes in riding gear, getting together for rides. But where? Merced. I looked again. *So they like their bikes up there.* The article mentioned they tried to get a club going with no success. Disbanded. As good a place as any to start. Might take some legwork to get it going but my instincts told me yes... *Merced, California, here I come.* The open road became a sanctuary for me long ago. A place to unwind, to contemplate, to be free. Heading to Merced was no exception. I could lay down roots and set up shop for a while. *Yep. Might be nice, see how I like it.*

I'd been married once to Catarina. Fresh out of high school and struggling to make ends meet. "You're too young to get married, Diego. Why don't you wait?" my sweet mother warned me, but we were blinded. I was nineteen at the time and I wanted what I wanted.

"Stay out of it. I love Catarina and she loves me. We're getting married." Five good years or so I'd thought. Put my heart and soul into it as a man. We thought we would never want to be apart from one another. *Fairytales don't last forever, sometimes they end badly.* A vivid flashback came to mind as I sat in Bakersfield.

"What the hell is going on? Get the fuck out of my house!" Some weedy dude was bumping and grinding with my wife. "Is this why you've been working late?" I screamed. I nearly lost my mind when I caught her.

"You were never home and I was lonely." Catarina's sad eyes filled with tears, staring back at me. The irony being I was working hard as a mechanic at my local garage trying to make ends meet. Catarina worked as a secretary in a doctor's office. The divorce sucked the life right out of me. Then add the drain on my little bank account and you could say I received the ultimate uppercut. After that, I vowed never to be committed again.

"I heard you're looking for members? I'm in, if you'll have me." That was the moment I joined the Outlaw Souls. Six years ago to the day and I never looked back. A brotherhood that would never abandon me, so I couldn't abandon them. I would support my fellow riders to the death.

Belly full and with a new resolve, I briefly looked over Merced on my phone. It was close to college campuses and the nearby Yosemite park. Good places to take day rides to.

I rode into Merced, California on a candy-coated sunset two-and-a-half hours later to start my new life and a new chapter.

2. MISTY

The size of a clenched fist. The one muscle that does all the work. The illustrious aorta and master of the pulmonary valve function. The door to the lower heart chamber, allowing the pulmonary artery to do its work, pumping blood through the body.

My eye vision was blurring because of all the back and forth over the textbook pages. I was tired from trying to absorb information and retain it for my upcoming test. I was getting back to basics first and revisiting my knowledge of myocardial infarctions. In layman's terms, the heart attack. I was knee-deep in the study zone with anatomy books spread open to various pages at my study desk in my room. The sun streamed through my curtains, making it a little more bearable. My mug of strong coffee helped that along as well.

Funny that scientists say the heart holds more intelligence than the brain. It's the epicenter of the body. If my heart had such intelligence, why was I always getting stabbed in it? It made me think of Carlos. I raised my head up from my books, giving myself an eye break, and sipped on my coffee. The guy was a heartbreaker and dream killer – that was what I called him. The suave Mexican with dark, jet-black hair, chiseled face and well-toned physique. He was older than me by three years. I didn't know any better when he wormed his way into my life.

"Hey, pretty lady. You're waiting on your brother, right?" That silky voice entered my life while I waited on Palo outside the clubhouse to give me a ride to my friend's house. When I looked at him, I thought he was mesmerizing. I thought he was a God. *My first mistake.*

We dated from the tender age of twenty-three on the low for three long years. He was part of the fucked-up motorcycle club – Las Balas. I shook my head at my stupidity as I listened to the birds chirp. As the hands of fate would have it, he left later down the track after we broke up. From that point on, I wanted nothing to do with Las Balas. Hard to deal with because my brother was involved with them, heavy.

"El Diablo's gone now. I can run the club the right way now." My older brother Palo had his sights set on being the next head of the club. He'd been riding with Las Balas a long time.

"I don't want nothing to do with the club. All that criminal activity is what Carlos was involved in. I'm studying to be a doctor and you need to keep that shit out of the house." My limits had been reached. The destruction and bloodshed that Las Balas caused was common knowledge to those in the know. I used to live with Carlos and got caught up in the lifestyle he provided. The cars, the bags, the shopping, the dinners and the sex. All that money could buy. Except it didn't stop him keeping his dick in his pants. I didn't know the extent of the cheating until we broke up.

It was exposed one night when I was out with my study

partners from campus. Another Spanish chica approached me at a local bar.

"Ola. I see what he likes." Her long dark hair swung as she walked. She had olive skin and wore a skintight dress. I was halfway wasted at the time so I was paying little attention to her.

"What?" I slurred back at her.

"You Carlos's girl?" The bar was cranking and I was ready to get back out on the dancefloor with my girls and this payasa was scanning me. Up and down. Up and down.

"Used to be. Not anymore." I could barely focus. I was that drunk. I was hanging onto the bar for support, laughing like a hyena. All I knew at that point was having fun. A damn good time in fact.

"I had him." She wiggled her manicured hand in my face. Then I watched as she turned and sashayed away. That happened a lot during the relationship, not just after the fact. But every time, Carlos sweet-talked me back off the ledge.

"Baby, she's lying. You can't believe nothing these chicas say." The pleading, the begging, and the puppy dog eyes. I somehow managed to take him back every time.

"No, it wasn't like that! I gave her a kiss on the cheek." He would always hunch his shoulders up like I was attacking him when I accused him. "You didn't see what you thought you saw." Toxic screaming matches followed pretty quickly after that. Some involved me throwing plates at his head. Blame it on my hot Spanish blood.

"*Estúpido!*" So the cycle continued where I cried and Carlos would wine and dine me right out of my clothes. Things would go back to being good for a few months. Like nothing happened.

"When you finish med school, you and I can get

married. We can have a family." The guy was a compulsive liar and fed lies like cotton candy to every woman he met.

Then I would inevitably hear through the grapevine that he was together with other girls. The last straw was when I caught him red-handed. I walked into the bedroom. I had to adjust my eyes at first. It was as if they didn't want to absorb what they were witnessing. A slender girl riding on top of him, moaning in the middle of the act. In *our* bedroom. My heart fell apart right then and there. Our sheets soiled by this heifer. Cheated on more times than I could remember.

I let out a deep sigh at the memory. Carlos, with his swarthy looks, was one that my brother actually approved of. And he didn't approve of many. So I left. Packed right in the middle of the night.

"Don't leave! We can work this out! It's not a big deal, my heart is with you."

The texts and phone calls came for weeks, trying to win me back. And that was how I ended up living at the other end of my brother's house. My brother got on my nerves sometimes so I thought it best to get my own place in due course.

"I feel responsible," Palo said when I wept in his arms. "You should come live with me for a while 'till you get back on your feet."

I wasn't going to live with my parents. I wanted peace and quiet to study. They were never quiet over there. After that, let's just say the next time I saw Carlos out he had a black eye. My brother Palo had fixed him up and told him to stop calling me. For the most part, he was protective over me.

"I want you to finish medical school. That's what you wanted to do. Follow your dreams," he told me.

That was why my room consisted mostly of medical books. Wall to wall in fact. Amongst some other crowd favorites when I had time to read them. Attending University of California's medical school left me very few hours for hobbies. But when I had time to party, it was on. I'd watched three of my loved ones pass on because of heart complications – misdiagnosed. In a lot of ways, my aspiration to be a heart surgeon stemmed from this. I wanted to be the one giving the right diagnosis. To walk in and tell the family.

"He's going to pull through. He made it." Not the dreaded doom and gloom like when my Uncle passed away. I would never forget the day. The doctor pulled down his teal mask with a grim face.

"Unfortunately, your Uncle didn't make it. We did our best." *No*. I didn't want to hear that anymore. I wanted to save lives. To help people. My family members weren't helping themselves though. They ate all sorts of heavy, rich, Puerto Rican foods. Part of my culture, no running from that with all our large family gatherings.

I happened to be the pioneering one in my family. The first one to go to college, a foreign concept to my extended family. They didn't understand why I couldn't be at every family gathering and doing things with them at every turn. I was looking forward to letting loose with my friends.

CLICK HERE To Continue

CONNECT WITH HOPE

Come hang out with the most amazing group of "Stoners" and join in on all the fun! This is an exclusive group where readers and fans of drama-filled, steamy romances come together to talk about Hope's books. This is the place to engage with other fans in a fun and inclusive way as well as get access to exclusive content, find out about new releases, giveaways, and contests, as well as vote on covers before anyone else and so much more!

CLICK HERE to join the Hope Stone Readers Group on Facebook.

ABOUT THE AUTHOR

Hope Stone is a contemporary romance author who loves writing hot and steamy, but also emotion-filled stories with twists and turns that keep readers guessing. Hope's books revolve around possessive alpha men who love protecting their sexy and sassy heroines. But enough of the boring stuff. ***How about we kick it up a notch because…***

The fun stuff, the juicy stuff, the REAL stuff is in the Facebook group! It's a judgement-free, safe and fun group where romance lovers can be themselves and the primary spot for me to let my freak flag fly!

WARNING: *If you're not a fan of laughing your ass off, seeing ridiculously hot biker dudes on the daily, or getting exclusive freebies then this group might not be for you.*

CLICK HERE to join the Hope Stone Readers Group on Facebook.